THE
FALL
OF THE
STONE
CITY

Born in 1936, Ismail Kadare is Albania's best-known poet and novelist. Translations of his novels have appeared in more than forty countries. In 2005 he was awarded the first Man Booker International Prize for 'a body of work written by an author who has had a truly global impact'. *The Fall of the Stone City* was shortlisted for the Independent Foreign Fiction Prize 2013. Ismail Kadare is the recipient of the highly prestigious 2009 Premio Príncipe de Asturias de las Letras in Spain.

'Both in his deployment of material and in his vision of life, Kadare is the equal of the often invoked Kafka'
Literary Review

'A masterful performance'
Daily Mail

'There are very few writers alive today with the depth, power and resonance of this remarkable novelist'
Herald

'*The Fall of the Stone City* is written with a persuasive lightness of touch'
Irish Times

'Mesmerizing... A well-crafted translation of a European masterpiece'
Booklist

'[Kadare] is on brilliant but unsettling form here'
Mail on Sunday

'Kadare tells it in agile and suspenseful detail'
Boston Globe

THE
FALL
OF THE
STONE
CITY

ISMAIL KADARE

TRANSLATED FROM THE ALBANIAN
BY JOHN HODGSON

CANONGATE
Edinburgh · London

This paperback edition first published by Canongate Books in 2013

www.canongate.tv

First published in Great Britain in 2012 by Canongate Books Ltd,
14 High Street, Edinburgh EH1 1TE

First published in Albania as *Darka e Gabuar* in 2008 by Onufri

British Library Cataloguing-in-Publication Data
A catalogue record for this book is available on
request from the British Library

ISBN 978 0 85786 012 5

Typeset in Bembo by Palimpsest Book Production Ltd,
Falkirk, Stirlingshire

Printed and bound by CPI Group (UK) Ltd, Croydon, CR0 4YY

PART ONE

1943

CHAPTER ONE

No sign of jealousy between Big Dr Gurameto and Little Dr Gurameto had ever been apparent. Although they bore the same surname they had no family connection and had it not been for medicine their destinies would surely never have become entwined; still less would they have acquired the labels "big" and "little", which created a relationship between them that doubtless neither desired.

It was as if a hidden hand had ensured that the city's two most famous surgeons could never be separated, even if they had wished, and moreover had created an equilibrium between them that would never be upset. Big Dr Gurameto was not only older and more imposing than his colleague but had studied gynaecology in Germany, definitely a larger and more formidable country than Italy, where Little Dr Gurameto had trained. Although the competition between the two was slow to surface, everybody was sure it existed, carefully concealed, and that one day it would burst out with noise and furore into the greatest medical rivalry the city had ever known.

Meanwhile both doctors, or rather the relationship between them, played a significant role in every public event. This was perhaps because the people found it hard to hold two members of the profession in equal esteem and could hardly wait for one to get the better of the other. So far, Big Dr Gurameto had claimed the victory on every occasion; although this might be too strong a phrase, just as it would be an exaggeration to call the other doctor the loser.

Four years earlier, the event that some people called *the Italian invasion* and others *Albania's unification with Italy* seemed designed specifically to upset the equilibrium between the two doctors and elevate one at the expense of the other. But the contest remained inconclusive: on one day the little doctor seemed certain to win, and on the next the big one. Little Dr Gurameto never gave anything away but Big Dr Gurameto's face wore an expression of suppressed fury. This made him look more imposing than ever. There was a lot of speculation as to why he should look so furious. A satirical paper finally identified his anger as a pale reflection of the rage reportedly felt by Adolf Hitler when his friend Benito Mussolini disembarked in Albania without telling him beforehand.

Finally, after the first confused weeks, Big Dr Gurameto had emerged with his authority enhanced. Some found this paradoxical while to others it was a logical thing because, quite apart from the Italian occupation and the infighting between the Duce and the Führer, Germany remained the senior ally. If Germany abandoned Italy, Little Dr Gurameto's country would be in the soup.

In the autumn of 1943 that is precisely what happened: Italy suddenly capitulated and lost her friend. Alliances have been broken throughout history but in this case the prospects for Italy were especially grim. To make matters worse, Italy's big German brother felt not the slightest pity but turned violently against her. Germany accused Italy of betrayal and showered her with insults and contempt. Germany's rage was uncontainable and German soldiers were ordered to shoot their former allies on the spot as deserters.

Events moved so fast that the city of Gjirokastër, accustomed to viewing the world in both broad and detailed perspective, seemed to lose its bearings. Its bewilderment was such that for the first time ever the city failed to interpret the situation in so far as it affected the two Dr Gurametos. The new balance of power after Italy's surrender should have offered an ideal opportunity to reassess the relationship between the men: Italy was on her knees, the German Army was advancing north from Greece to fill the vacuum left in Albania and Big Dr Gurameto and Little Dr Gurameto were going about the city as always. But the chance was missed. The city's inhabitants shook their heads, sighed and reached the philosophical conclusion that this oversight was surest proof of the dramatic nature of the events.

The longer people pondered the political situation, the more complicated and even mysterious it seemed. Italy had capitulated, as everybody knew, but what was the status of Albania? Either she had capitulated together with Italy or some other interpretation was called for, and the more one tried to explain the situation, the more confused it became.

Sometimes the question was put more simply. Albania had been one of the three component parts of the now fallen empire. Did this mean that one third of Germany's fury would fall on her?

It was not easy to find the answer. Any fool could see that Italy was bearing the brunt of Germany's anger but nobody could forecast what would happen to the other two parts of the empire, Ethiopia and Albania. But then, who else but the Albanians could be the targets of German rage? The German Army was less than forty miles away. Germany was surely drooling at the mouth, like a wolf that has caught sight of a lamb.

A feeling of helplessness had the city in its grip when an unexpected development put an end to all uncertainty. One morning two unknown aircraft dropped thousands of leaflets over Gjirokastër. They were in two languages, German and Albanian, and provided a full explanation. Germany was not invading, she merely wanted to pass through Albania. She was coming as a friend. Not only did Germany have no quarrel with Albania, in fact she was liberating the country from the hated Italian occupation and restoring Albania's violated independence. She recognised ethnic Albania with Kosovo and Çamëria within its borders.

Despite this reassurance some sceptics came out with the familiar refrain. "How can those high-ups tell what's happening down here?" By "high-ups" they implied both high-level German officials and the aircraft dropping the leaflets. Yet the city's nightmare did seem finally to be over. People could not believe their eyes, although the text was plain and moreover in two languages. It was almost too good to be true.

With calmer minds people began offering their opinions

of the leaflets. As always, these were divided. Some liked this form of advance notice, so untypical of the deviousness of modern life. "Nowadays some almighty state can cross your border at night like a thief and protest the next morning without a flicker of shame, 'It was you who attacked me.' This prior warning in broad daylight is totally transparent, indeed gentlemanly, like sending a visiting card."

"Nonsense," said others. "This visiting card business is precisely the worst possible insult to any country, especially a brave country like ours. 'Albania, I'm coming tomorrow morning. Come out to welcome me at ten o'clock. Never mind what people say about me. Take no notice of my artillery and tanks, because Germany is good, and brings culture and bouquets of flowers.' Are you witless enough to believe this twaddle?"

"At least visiting cards are preferable to bombs," said the others in self-defence.

A third group, sticklers for rules and regulations, raised another concern. Their anxiety was of a special kind, as fastidious in its demands as an overfed tomcat, arrogant and somehow brazen. "All right, so Germany has stated her intentions, but what stand will Albania take?"

This question created a sense of unease. "Rather than being finicky we should thank God the Germans haven't torn us to shreds like they did the Greeks." Various proverbs were cited in illustration, especially the one about the starved goat with its tail held high.

Meanwhile those with more patience urged caution. They produced some flyers they had found, left on their doorsteps overnight. These were not such attractive productions as the leaflets that had fallen from the air. They were in only one language and were the opposite of the leaflets in every respect. The flyers called for war and nothing but war, and vilified the Germans as evil invaders, worse even than the Italians.

People grew suspicious and gave the matter more consideration. Apparently there were two schools of thought in Albania as a whole. This fact made little impression on Gjirokastër. Everybody knew that there had been occasions when the city thought itself wiser than the rest of the country, and this case called for her wisdom, because it would fall to Gjirokastër, as the first large city through which the Germans would pass, to deal with them before anyone else.

CHAPTER TWO

The city had always had a reputation for arrogance. There were different explanations for this. Viewed in the most charitable light, its pride was an aspect of its isolation. The supporters of this theory, conscious of its obvious inadequacy, would hasten to add that "isolation" in this context required some qualification. The city was surrounded by a far-reaching hinterland with which it was on poor terms and the inhabitants of this hinterland considered the city alien, if not their actual enemy. At its back to the north, among the endless mountains full of foxes and wolves, lay the rugged and apparently innumerable villages of Labëria. To the east beyond the river and its valley lay the villages of Lunxhëria, which were also irritating to the city but for the opposite reason: because of their gentleness. Then there were the Greek-minority villages stretched along both sides of the river valley to the south. The Greek peasants who worked the land as sharecroppers were treated with disdain but perhaps provoked the city even more. The subtle irritation they caused was felt more during the hours of sleep than by day, and there was no reason for it at all. The presence of these Greeks was like a temptation to sin, leading the residents of the city into prejudiced opinions against not only the Greeks, but Hellenism as a whole, the state of Greece, its politics, and even its language.

To complicate this patchwork further, in the very middle of the territory, or more precisely between the city and the Greek-minority area, lay Lazarat, the most stubborn and vicious village imaginable. Historians, unable to account for its rancour towards Gjirokastër, said only that this malice did no harm, as long as the city bore the brunt of it and prevented it from seeping further into Albania.

It was said that on dark nights the lights of Gjirokastër, though faint and distant, so irked the villagers of Lazarat that they fired guns in the direction of the stone city.

According to other more cautious chroniclers, the origin of this enmity lay in the tall houses in whose upper storeys the ladies of the city were believed to live. Behind the roughcast walls, the ladies observed their own unbending rituals. Rarely seen in public, they were the city's secret rulers.

The city itself was inured to all this and sought neither conciliation nor agreement with anyone. Faced with such general hostility, any other city might perhaps have attempted to ally itself with one neighbour against another, for instance with Labëria against the Greek minority or Lazarat against Lunxhëria. But Gjirokastër was not as wise as it should have been. Or perhaps it was wiser. It came to the same thing.

Not only did the city refuse conciliation, as a warning it illuminated its prison at night. This prison was inside the castle, at the stone city's highest point. With this baleful light, which travellers compared to a malignant version of the floodlit Acropolis of Athens, Gjirokastër sent its message to its entire hinterland, Labëria, Lazarat, Lunxhëria, and the Greeks: here you will all rot, without distinction, without mercy.

This threat was not an idle one if one remembered the three hundred imperial judges – unemployed since the fall of the Ottoman Empire – who bided their time at home.

The reinstatement of these pitiless judges would turn even the most sweet-tempered of cities, let alone Gjirokastër, into a wild beast. People were heard to say that if even Lunxhëria exerted her charms in vain, nothing could mollify this city. The lights of the churches of Lunxhëria twinkled and their bells pealed at Easter and their women and their freshwater springs were of rare sweetness. The stone city was not as blind as it appeared; it took note of everything. Sometimes girls or young brides vanished from the villages of Lunxhëria. Their neighbours searched for them everywhere, in the streams, in ravines and among the shepherds' shielings. Eventually a soft sigh like the rustle of silk would suggest firmly that they must have ended up in the tall houses of the city.

It was never proved whether men of the city had in fact abducted these women. Were the girls kidnapped or had they drifted like butterflies, of their own free will, close to the formidable gates of the houses, until one day they were sucked in, never to emerge again. Nobody knew what went on inside. Were they wretched there or happy? Perhaps their dream of becoming ladies had come true. Or perhaps they themselves had been only a dream, and nothing else.

This was how things stood just before the Germans arrived. The old conviction that Albania, when faced with danger, would come to its senses and forget its internal strife proved ill-founded.

Three days before the vanguard of the Wehrmacht crossed the state frontier, the situation was as follows. The villages of Lunxhëria with their sweet springs and lovely girls closed in on themselves and seemed determined to take no notice of the Germans. Their main concern in any invasion was the forcible seizure of brides; the reports that the Germans were not noted for this (and indeed, at least according to the leaflets dropped from the sky, would respect the traditional Albanian virtues) was sufficient to allay any fears of what would come from foreign occupation.

The Greek minority, seeing that this army had crushed the state of Greece, kept their heads down and prayed to God they would not be noticed. But for the villagers of Lazarat, the very fact that the Germans had thrashed the Greeks, whom they could not abide under any circumstances, was enough if not to arouse their admiration, at least to soften any animosity against the aggressors.

In Labëria the situation was different. The villagers' opinions for or against communism were transformed instantly into feelings for or against the Germans. As always, when they ran out of arguments they reached for their guns. As they had more bullets than words there was little chance of an end to the quarrel.

The same questions that were fought over with such commotion and brutality in the villages of Labëria were debated more delicately in the city of Gjirokastër itself. In its elegant third-floor drawing rooms, binoculars were passed from hand to hand to observe the main road along which "the war was coming".

There were two schools of thought. As expected, the communists were calling for war, fervently, and soon. The nationalists were not opposed to war but were not inclined to either fervour or haste. In their view excessive zeal was more characteristic of Russia than Albania and there was no reason why Albania should rush into war blindly, without considering her own advantage. Germany was indeed an invader, but Red Russia was no better. Besides, Germany was bringing home Kosovo and Çamëria, while Russia offered nothing but collective farms. In contrast, the words "ethnic Albania" in the German leaflets not only failed to conciliate the communists but actually provoked them. Their impatience for war probably did come from Russia. This was only natural for they were led by two or three Serbian chiefs for whom the phrase "ethnic Albania" was a red rag and worse.

These opinions changed with every passing hour and were expressed most bluntly in the city's cafés. On one sentiment everyone could agree. Pass through, Mr Germany, like you promised, in transit. Don't provoke us, and we won't provoke you. Achtung! You've already thrashed Greece and Serbia. That's your business! Give us Kosovo and Çamëria, jawohl!

Of all these predictions, the worst came true. On the highway at the entrance to the city the German advance party was fired on. It was neither war nor appeasement, just an ambush. The three motorcyclists of the advance party made a sharp U-turn and sped back in the direction from which they had come. The shooters also vanished, as if swallowed up by the bushes.

The news soon reached the city's cafés and everybody scrambled for the shelter of their own homes. As they hurried off they exchanged parting shots, some reviling the communists for staging a provocation and then scarpering, as they did so often, and others denouncing the cowards who would stop at nothing to appease the wolf.

Even before the heavy gates of the houses closed, the news had spread: the city would be punished for its treachery. What stunned everybody was not the punishment itself, but the way it would be carried out. It was an unusual reprisal: the city was to be blown up. Of course this was frightening, but the first response was not fear but shame.

It took some time to sink in. The stone houses with their title deeds, the three hundred imperial judges, the houses of the ladies and with them the ladies themselves with their silken nightdresses, their secrets and their bangles, would fly into the air and fall from the sky like hail.

As if to avert their eyes from this appalling vision, the citizens fell back on their recent quarrels. "Look what the communists have done to us." "It's your own fault. You thought you'd won Kosovo and Çamëria." "It wasn't us, it was you, pretending you would fight." "What, so we'd do the fighting while you stood back and watched?" "We didn't say we'd fight, you did. You lied." "You're on the warpath? Stay where you are. Fight, or sit tight, just don't move!"

In this way they snapped at each other until the argument eventually returned to the unresolved matter of who had fired on the Germans. The silence that followed was wearisome, and so back they came to the manner of their punishment: being blown up. This was of course an appalling prospect, but the men of the city felt there was something unspeakably and particularly shameful about it. Cities everywhere had been punished down the ages, and indeed, if you thought hard, this had been the number one calamity throughout history. Cities had been besieged, deprived of food and water and bombarded; their gates had been battered, their walls demolished, their houses burned to ashes and flattened, their sites ploughed and sown with salt so that no grass would ever grow again. Many cities have met their end, despairing, but with courage. To be blown up was something else.

Finally, the men understood where their feeling of shame came from. This reprisal seemed to them an insult to their manhood. "Isn't this a sort of punishment for women?" went the talk round the tables. "Or am I wrong?" The essential idea was easy to grasp instinctively but hard to explain. Being blown into the air and made to leap and caper — all this was women's stuff. In short, the stone city, so proud of its manly traditions, had been marked out to die like a woman. How delighted the despised villages around the city would be. Or would they feel sorry for Gjirokastër? In any event it would be too late.

At this point the men's hearts sank and their voices failed. They turned their heads away so as not to burst into tears like the women, who, being women, were already weeping.

★

In the gathering dusk something for which there was still no word crept over the city.

Those who were determined to flee left for the villages of Lunxhëria or the Broad Mountain, where they thought the wolves and foxes would be more hospitable.

The rattle of the approaching tanks could be heard and after waiting so long, many people thought that this protracted roar was the explosion, a newly-invented way of being blown up, German-style.

Finally the German tanks appeared, moving in a black, orderly file along the highway. The first tank halted at the river bridge, rotated its turret and aimed its barrel at the city. The second, third, fourth and all the others did the same, in sequence.

Even before the first shell was fired, Gjirokastër's inhabitants had understood not only the tanks' message but the whole situation. The stone city had fired on the German Army's advance guard. Now it would be punished according to the rules of war, which took no account of how cultivated, ancient or crazy a town might be.

The first shell flew through the air above the roofs just as an old man of the Karagjoz house announced, "I'll not be blown up, I'll make a dash for it before you blink. But this is torture, neither one thing nor the other!"

The shells fell first on the outskirts and then by careful degrees approached the centre and people in the shelters made their final wishes, uttered what they thought were their last words, prayed.

Then the bombardment suddenly stopped. The first inquisitive people who emerged from the cellars were astonished to find the city still there and not in ruins as they had imagined. But this fact was easy to grasp compared to the next piece of news, which concerned the cessation of the shelling and was strange and baffling. One of the inhabitants had apparently waved a white sheet from a rooftop, nobody could tell exactly where. He had signalled to the Germans the city's surrender. While lots of people accepted this as truth, many thought it must have been a mirage.

Meanwhile the rumble of the tanks had started again. Now they were slowly climbing towards Gjirokastër.

Dusk fell at last and under the cover of darkness harder questions were asked. Who had raised the white flag? The original question of who had fired on the German advance party now seemed naive and childish. People sensed that it would soon be answered and plenty of men would boast of this feat, while whoever had waved the white sheet would vanish into obscurity.

There was no way of identifying the man or even the house from whose roof the flag had been raised. "Somewhere in that direction," hazarded those who claimed to have seen it. Other people tried to guess who it might have been but when asked to pin down his name, or at least the roof, they all shrugged their shoulders as if this shame, if that is what it could be called, was too great to be borne by a single person, or a single roof.

Everybody agreed on this and so they felt relieved when someone found an explanation for what had happened, one that dispelled every suspicion of blame. The explanation was very simple: no search would ever discover the person or ghost who had raised the flag of surrender. The September wind had pulled a white curtain out of a window left

CHAPTER THREE

Events had so stunned the city that it was hard to believe that this was still the same day. The very word "afternoon" seemed not to fit any more. Should it be called the second part of the day? The last part? Perhaps the most treacherous part, harbouring a centuries-old grudge against the day as a whole, or rather its first part, which you might call fore-noon; forget the idea of morning. Its malice had rankled, to erupt suddenly that mid-September.

There was also a sense of gratitude to destiny for at least having preserved the city from other long-forgotten calamities such as the Double Night, a sort of calendrical monster that beggared the imagination, a stretch of time that was unlike anything else and came from no one knew where, from the bowels of the universe perhaps, a union of two nights in one, smothering the day between them as dishonoured women once were smothered in the old houses of Gjirokastër.

Recourse to such flights of fancy was understandable because the inhabitants of the city had lost something that had always been a source of pride to them: their cool heads. Or had they lost their heads altogether?

Nevertheless, with whatever mental powers left to them

they hoped they had grasped certain things. For instance they understood that they had exchanged being blown up for a mass shooting but they didn't yet know who would be the unfortunate people marked out for death. No doubt talks were under way with the Germans about their demands but nobody could work out where these were taking place, or who was talking to whom. Instead, people pricked their ears to catch the scraping sounds of footsteps in the night. Perhaps these were intermediaries, or would-be denunciators who did not know where to go.

Meanwhile another kind of sound was heard. It was more than unexpected. It was incredible, like the story of the man caught in the wolf's fangs who in despair had prayed, "Oh God, make this a dream!" and whose prayer was answered. The sound was indeed like an answer to prayer, a happy end to an inauspicious beginning. It resembled machine-gun fire of a totally different kind, as if a new sort of weapon had been invented, one which fired music.

"What sort of gun is this? It's like the music of Strauss," said the Shamet boys, who played in the municipal band. Moreover, it was apparent at once that this noise, whether gunfire, music or both, did not come from the city's main square but from the . . . from the house of Big Dr Gurameto.

Before they concluded that Dr Gurameto had lost his wits, something else made people catch their breath. It was the feeling of bottomless and boundless remorse that follows an unpardonable oversight: they had forgotten the two doctors.

How had this happened? In all the upheaval of these

world-shaking events with the rise and fall of states, broken alliances and changes to frontiers and flags, how had they forgotten the two doctors, who particularly should have been remembered at such a time? Forgetting their rivalry, their points of comparison and the fluctuating authority of each was like losing a compass bearing, forgetting the city's barometer or thermometer; not to mention the stock-market index and the currency devaluation and the collapse of the Swiss banks that would follow a German invasion. In short, the mainspring that ticks inside every city and whose ticking everyone feels without knowing where it might be had been broken.

And now it seemed that Big Dr Gurameto was taking his revenge. "So you forgot me, did you? Now just see if I don't drive you crazy!" And in the silence he had turned on his gramophone to wake the heavens. But this supposition, like most speculations that are too hasty, was soon questioned. Revenge was not Dr Gurameto's style. Everyone knew he stood aloof from all these things.

So what was happening in his house? Any idiot could hear the music. But what it was for, for what occasion or what purpose, nobody could tell.

At once two new theories were put forward. The first claimed that Dr Gurameto's intention was to cock a snook at the Germans. "So you're invading us? You think you've frightened us and brought us to our knees? Nothing of the sort! Look, in front of your very nose my daughter's getting engaged and I'm not postponing the party because according to our customs no Albanian will put off even the hour let alone the day of a celebration. So I'm behaving as if you weren't here at all. You're even welcome to come if you like. According to our traditions, my house is open to everyone, friend or foe."

This interpretation showed what a fine man Big Dr Gurameto was and a cheer went up, if a silent one. "Bravo for Big Dr Gurameto, the toast of Gjirokastër!' Simultaneously everyone derided his counterpart, Little Dr Gurameto. "Down with the little one! To hell with him, a disgrace to the neighbourhood and our whole city!"

But this conjecture proved short-lived. It was next reported that Dr Gurameto was not holding an engagement party. His dinner was not intended as a slap in the Germans' faces. On the contrary, he was hosting it in their honour. He had invited these foreigners in order to say, "They greeted you with bullets at the gates of the city this morning, but I'll welcome you with food and wine and music!"

A storm of fury blew up against the doctor. Many people said they had always known he would be unmasked as the Germanophile he was and others cursed him as the Judas of the city. They were correspondingly profuse in their praise for Little Dr Gurameto. At least the little one was cowering in the dark like everybody else, long-suffering but heroic, the pride of all Albania, whether Greater Albania or not!

It was plain to see that not a peep came from the darkened house of Little Dr Gurameto, while the big doctor's house was ablaze with light, the music grew louder and above its strains the shouts of toasts and cheers in German could be heard.

The big doctor's supporters, eager to exonerate him from this charge of treason, resorted to the suspicion that his mind had given way. Someone in this story had obviously lost his wits but nobody could tell if it was the doctor, the Germans or both.

Meanwhile, to spite the doctor's admirers, the anti-Big Gurameto faction, more venomous than ever, asserted that the music was interspersed with machine-gun fire and that hostages were already being killed, not in the city square but in the cellars of the doctor's house.

Others went even further, claiming that hostages the Germans especially wanted, such as Jakoel the Jew, were being led out of the cellars to be shot then and there in the dining hall, for sport! In other words, shoot them, slice open their bodies on the table, remove the organs for brave German soldiers and raise a toast to Albanian–German friendship.

This extravagant fantasy, especially the vision of Big Dr Gurameto with his surgical instruments cutting up bodies during dinner, brusquely restored people to their senses and the city thereby regained the faculty on which it had prided itself for the last six centuries at least.

It was true, though, that Dr Gurameto's house was brightly lit and echoed to the sounds of merriment, with Brahms followed by Lili Marlene. And at the same time, machine guns were being lined up in the city square and trained on hostages handcuffed in pairs, who shivered in the dampness of the night. The weather was cold. A bitter north wind blew down the Gorge of Tepelene, as it always did when destiny took a turn for the worse. The hostages stood waiting. No gun had yet fired and the helmeted soldiers now and then lifted their heads in surprise towards the music. But it was the hostages who were the most bewildered and uncomprehending as they listened.

There could be no more extreme opposites than that grim square with its expectation of death and Big Dr Gurameto's house with its singing and champagne, yet soon, inexplicably, it was assumed that the machine guns and the music, however far apart they might be, were mysteriously linked. But what was the connection between them, and did it promise good or ill?

As the sound of the gramophone slowly faded, so did the anguish of speculation about the dinner. The city could recall many extraordinary banquets of all kinds down the centuries, some joyful and others disgusting: guests had tried to throw themselves from the rooftops in their euphoria, had fired at each other in mid-celebration or attempted to kidnap the lady of the house; dawn had broken to reveal hosts and guests poisoned together. Yet none could be compared to the dinner of this night.

Reaching back deeper into the past, people remembered Christ's Last Supper, as told by the scriptures, and were sure they would find the answer there. But as soon as they felt they had hit upon the truth, it eluded them again. Clearly, neither Big Dr Gurameto nor any of his German guests were Christ, but it would be going too far to identify either with Judas. With a sigh and a prayer to the Lord to forgive them these sinful thoughts, they tried to empty their minds completely.

Among the scattered houses of outlying neighbourhoods fresh news was slow to arrive so people made do with the old. Even an hour later they were still arguing about machine guns making music. Shaqo Bej Kokoboja, who had once found himself on the Prussian–Russian front by mistake, said that all this talk was nonsense: he had felt the bullets of a Schwarzlose machine gun on his own back and its sound was as familiar to him as his old lady's snoring. When others retorted that nobody was talking about those old First World War blunderbusses but about Schubert – ever heard of Schubert? – he lost his temper. "Give over, all those Schuberts or sherbets are just popguns. Don't tell me a machine gun can do a foxtrot or a cannon can play an opera."

In one of these isolated houses a dinner was recollected from the distant past. Its memory had been preserved down the generations like a legend or a children's bedtime story. The tale concerned the master of a house who was bound by a promise to invite a stranger to dinner. He handed the dinner invitation to his son with instructions. The son set off in search of an unknown passer-by but became frightened on the lonely road. Passing the cemetery, he threw the invitation over the wall and ran through the darkness, not knowing that the invitation had fallen on a grave. He returned home and said to his father, "I've done what you told me." At that moment there appeared at the door the dead man with the invitation in his hand. The father and his family shrank back in horror. "You invited me and I've come," said the dead man. "Don't stare at me like that!"

Meanwhile, the dinner at Dr Gurameto's continued. Nobody knew what was happening inside the house until news of a different kind spread, this time as welcome as an April breeze. It floated gently, more delicate than a rainbow, vulnerable to the slightest current. The irresistible wind from the Gorge of Tepelene seemed to help carry it to its proper destination: the hostages were being freed.

The news was breathtaking; people could not get it

into their skulls. The hostages were . . . the hostages were not being shot, but released. They had not fallen, shredded by bullets in the city square. They were slipping away, one by one, each to their own home. Oh God! It was Big Dr Gurameto who had performed this miracle!

The wave of gratitude towards him was uncontainable. Hearts melted, knees gave way, heads bowed. The heads then lifted to raise a proper cheer for Big Dr Gurameto. Never before had the mania for comparison, exalting one at the expense of the other, undergone such a reversal. The whole city felt bound to fall to its knees before Big Dr Gurameto, to wash his feet with tears and beg pardon for having doubted him. At the same time it was obliged to turn against his rival, the little doctor, this Judas of Europe and the continent's disgrace, who had rejoiced prematurely at their hero's downfall.

The little doctor was mystified. He and his supporters understood nothing of what was going on. Little Dr Gurameto had never nurtured any ill will against his colleague, and had always shown him every respect. But this in no way affected the violent movement of the barometer, which seemed to put paid to every nagging suspicion and conclude this long history of carefully hidden rivalry.

After settling accounts with Little Dr Gurameto, people returned, as was to be expected, to the central issue. As they gazed adoringly at Big Dr Gurameto's brightly lit house, the music coming from it sounded divine and the ancient building itself resembled less a house than a cathedral.

The old curiosity about the secrets of the city's ladies now quietly revived, if feebly after such a long abeyance. Was it true that Mrs Gurameto and her daughter were waltzing with the Germans, whose commanding officer, Baron von Schwabe, wore a mask?

This curiosity was bound sooner or later to settle again on the first, unavoidable question. What was this occasion really about? Some still called it the "dinner of shame" but others referred to it as the "resurrection dinner". The secret was finally coming out, conveyed through mysterious channels, perhaps carried by servants or the dispatch riders who came and went all night.

CHAPTER FOUR

And what happened was this: on the afternoon that preceded the dinner, after the tanks and armoured vehicles had rumbled and rattled their way into the town, there stepped out from one of the military cars onto the city square Colonel Fritz von Schwabe, commander of the German division and bearer of the Iron Cross. His legs still stiff, he stood surveying the scene and announced, "Gjirokastër. I have a friend here."

His aides thought he was joking but the colonel went on in the same tone of voice, "A great friend, from university, my closest friend, more than a brother to me."

His aides expected laughter to follow this statement. "I was joking," he would surely say, and explain himself.

But nothing of the sort happened. On the contrary, he gave his aides a look of the kind they had never seen and told them his friend's name. He mentioned the college in Munich where they had studied together and his address. "Big Dr Gurameto. Der grosse Doktor Gurameto, 22 Varosh Straße, Gjirokastër, Albanien."

The aides heard their commander order this Albanian to be found and brought to him at once.

Four soldiers mounted two motorcycles with sidecars.

Armed with machine guns, they sped off with the address of the man they were looking for.

At this point the town's inhabitants still had not emerged from the shelters, so nobody saw the soldiers knock at Dr Gurameto's gate and escort him away.

At the city square the colonel's aides finally believed what he had told them, but as they noticed how anxiously he waited for the man he claimed to be his friend, their suspicions were roused again. Was he really a great friend, closer than any brother, or someone wanted for arrest? They waited to see whether this famous doctor would be given a medal or shot for some crime, of what sort nobody could say.

The motorcycles returned, first one, then the other. All eyes were now focused on the mysterious doctor. Apparently the man would be neither decorated nor executed. This was something harder to credit: a sentimental reunion, as if from the last century or even the age of chivalry.

At first the doctor stood nonplussed and failed to recognise his college friend. Perhaps it was the passage of time, his military uniform or the two scars on his face. But then the meeting went as it should.

The doctor and the colonel embraced and their tears of emotion finally dispelled every shred of doubt. Such a touching encounter, so . . . no, no, it couldn't be of that kind. Neither of them seemed that sort. And yet there was something behind this. Colonel von Schwabe, although young and of relatively modest rank, had strong connections in Berlin, the capital of the Reich. He might know things that nobody else did, for instance that this doctor was about to be appointed the governor of Albania.

The emotional reunion continued, as touching as the discovery of a lost brother in an old ballad.

"Like the *Nibelungenlied*, eh? Or the *Kanun of Lekë Dukagjini*? Do you remember what you told me in the Widow Martha's Tavern? About Albanian honour, hospitality?"

"Remember it? Of course I do!" Big Dr Gurameto replied. He was overcome by nostalgia too, but now and then an inexplicable shadow crossed his face.

The colonel also looked pensive.

"I've dreamed of this meeting for so long," he said. "I used to talk to people about you and the things you told me. I used to read Karl May's adventure stories about Albania. People thought I was crazy. They didn't know how close we were. You know, when I believed I was on my deathbed I thought of you. I even had the delusion that it wasn't our military surgeon operating on me, but you. Do you remember telling me about that terrifying dream you had, in which you were operating on yourself? I dreamed that you were operating on me. The instruments were in someone else's hand, but I dreamed it was you who restored me to life. You brought me back from the grave."

The colonel broke off and laid his hand on one of the scars on his forehead. When he spoke again, his voice was slow, almost heartbroken. "And so when they gave me orders to take this tank division and occupy Albania, my first thought was of you. I wouldn't invade Albania but save it, unite it with the eternal Reich and of course, before anything else, I would find you, my brother. And I set off happily to the country where honour rules, as you used to say."

His voice faltered and he fell silent for a moment. "Dr Gurameto, they fired on me in your city."

His voice was now hoarse and he frowned. Big Dr Gurameto stood frozen to the spot.

"I was fired on," the colonel went on. "I was betrayed. The advance party barely escaped with their lives. When they told me, my first thought was again of you. It was my fault for believing you. Nostalgia had turned me soft and without thinking I had put my men in mortal danger. I was beside myself. 'Gurameto,' I shouted, 'you traitor, where's your Albanian honour now?'"

The doctor stood transfixed, speechless. The colonel's voice grew faint.

"I sent you word. I dropped thousands of leaflets from the air. I told you I was coming as a guest. I asked the master of the house, 'Will you receive guests?' And then came your reply. My men escaped by the skin of their teeth. When I saw my soldiers bent low over their motorcycles, I almost howled. All those things we talked about at the Widow Martha's Tavern, did they mean nothing? Where is your honour, Dr Gurameto? Have you nothing to say?"

The doctor finally found his voice. "I didn't fire on you, Fritz."

"Really? It was worse than that. Your country fired on me."

"I answer for my own house, not the state."

"It comes to the same."

"It doesn't come to the same. I'm not Albania, just as you're not Germany, Fritz. We're something else."

The colonel lowered his eyes thoughtfully. "Something else," he murmured. "Well put. You're an amazing man,

Gurameto. You always were special. You're the superman, aren't you? You don't belong to the real world."

"Nor do you, Fritz."

"You mean that's why we don't get on with the rest?"

"Perhaps. I'm still the person I was."

"And I'm not? You mean that this uniform of mine, these scars, the war, the Iron Cross have changed me? I tell you, they haven't, not in the slightest."

"If that's true, Fritz, and if you're still the same person, I'm inviting you to dinner at my house, according to the customs we spoke about. Tonight."

The colonel raised his hand to his scarred brow, as if struck by a blow. His icy stare seemed to say, "Come to dinner, in this country where they fired on me behind my back?"

He put his arms round Gurameto but this time his embrace was cold. Gurameto interpreted it as a refusal of his invitation and tensed his neck. But the reply was the opposite. Their final words were partly in Albanian and partly in archaic German.

As evening fell on the city, Big Dr Gurameto felt the weight of a sorrow he had never known before. He listened to the sounds of preparation for the dinner and looked out from the first floor veranda towards the gate of his yard, where his guest would knock.

The colonel came at the promised time and, strangely, his car drew up without a sound, as if it had glided through the air above the city to avoid being seen by anybody.

His guest seemed to have arrived so stealthily that the master of the house asked him if he should draw the curtains and turn off the gramophone.

To his surprise, the colonel said no. Certainly not. Wherever Colonel Fritz von Schwabe goes for dinner, especially in Albania, let the lamps be lit and the music sound, as custom demands. "You invited me to dinner, and here I am," his voice boomed.

Smiling, he bounded up the staircase, followed by his aides and a soldier carrying a case of champagne. They entered the great drawing room, kissed the hands of the lady and daughter of the house and gave a curt nod to the doctor's prospective son-in-law.

The slight embarrassment on both sides, perhaps because this was the first time any Albanian house had welcomed German servicemen, vanished at once when the guests took their places at the dinner table. Clearly the evening would go well. Cheerful toasts were raised. The conversation flowed without longueurs and paused without stalling. The colonel and his host sometimes talked tête-à-tête, teasing each other with recollections of student days, which inevitably involved the names of drinks and young ladies. Mrs Gurameto's sparkling eyes showed that this did not offend her in the slightest. Following the tradition of university feasts, the guests were provided with masks, which they wore or set aside as the fancy took them.

"My God," sighed the colonel. His voice was not loud, but a silence fell. "My God," he repeated, "for weeks, months, I've dreamed of visiting a house like this."

His expression clouded over again. His voice softened, as it had that afternoon in the city square.

"For so many weeks, so many months," he continued softly, "as I crossed the wasteland of Europe, with death and hatred all around me, I yearned for a dinner like this. Of all the possible houses in this whole sorry continent that I dreamed of visiting, yours was the very first."

"I believe you," Gurameto replied calmly.

"Thank you, brother. The prospect was doubly inviting, because the house was yours, and because it was Albanian. It was just as you said, like in *Lekë Dukagjini*: 'Give me your word of honour, oh master of the house!' What a magnificent phrase. The whole time I was thinking, quite rightly, that our ancient German customs are close to yours. The world has forgotten these customs, but we will bring them back. That's what I told myself, as I travelled across wintry, frozen Europe. It was all ours, we were winning all the time, but something was missing."

One of the officers tried to seize the opportunity of the silence to raise a toast, but at a glance from his superior he left his glass where it stood.

"And so, as I told you, when the order came to occupy— I mean to unite Albania, my first thought was that I would visit my brother. I would find him wherever he was. And look, I have come. But you . . . You fired on me, Gurameto. Treacherously, behind my back."

"It wasn't me," the doctor said quietly.

"I know. But you know better than I do that your *Kanun of Lekë Dukagjini* demands blood for blood. German blood was spilt. Blood is never counted as lost."

Dr Gurameto awaited the verdict with his eyes closed.

"Eighty hostages will wash away that blood. While we are dining here, my men are rounding them up."

The expression of the master of the house turned to stone. He had heard something about this, but had thought the order would be rescinded.

Everybody waited to hear how he would reply. That rigid face would produce something. For instance he might say, "Why tell me this?" Or, "You are my guest. Show me the respect that I have shown you." Or he might simply pronounce the old formula that followed an insult to a table, according to the *Kanun of Lekë Dukagjini*, and go to the window to announce to the people that his German guest had violated his hospitality.

But Big Dr Gurameto said nothing of the sort. The thought in his mind was of something entirely different.

In fact it was not a thought at all but a sudden, incongruous flashback of the strange dream of which the colonel had reminded him a few hours before on the city square. Instantaneously and with blinding clarity he saw himself stretched out on the operating table. He looked up – the surgeon operating on him was himself. This came as a surprise to him but what struck him most was the expression on the surgeon's face. It did not reveal whether the surgeon recognised him or not. Gurameto even wanted to say to him, "It's me, don't you know me?" But at that moment the surgeon, with the scalpel in his hand, gave a slight sign of recognition, as if this patient were a person he had met before. Again, Gurameto wanted to say, "Careful, be gentle, don't you see it's me, your own self?" But the surgeon donned his protective mask and Gurameto could only try to interpret the expression of this mask. It changed, sometimes suggesting that the surgeon would be gentle, as if to himself, but at other times the masked face conveyed the opposite impression, that he was the last person from whom Gurameto could expect kindness.

Gurameto wanted to question the surgeon but the

anaesthetic prevented him. The expression of the mask grew sterner. It seemed to say, now that you're in my hands, you'll see what I'll do to you. The torture continued. The mask bent over him. As the surgeon was about to make the first incision, he whispered, "Don't you know that a person's worst enemy is his own self?"

The colonel was talking at the dinner table but his voice came as if from a distance. The doctor could not be sure if he heard him correctly. "You brought me back to life, Gurameto." His voice was soft, very faint. "You brought me back to life, but to your own misfortune."

Of course this evening was his misfortune. From now on the whole city would revile him as a traitor. In the days, months and years to come, even after his death, this was how he would be remembered.

He wanted to wake from this nightmare too, but what came from his mouth were only a few calm words. "Fritz, free the hostages."

The dinner table froze.

"*Was?*"

The master of the house looked forlornly at his guest. "Free the hostages, Fritz," he repeated. "Libera obsides."

"How dare you?" A lump in the colonel's throat strangled his words. "How dare you give me orders. If you weren't . . . "

The colonel left the phrase unsaid, but everyone knew what he wanted to say. If you weren't my old college friend, from that tavern on the other side of ravaged Europe, there would be Armageddon here.

The colonel put his hand on Dr Gurameto's shoulder, as if comforting someone in shock. In a gentle, soothing voice and with a playful smile, he said, "You gave me an order in a dead language. What did you mean by that, my friend?"

The officers at the table stared wide-eyed, moving their hands from their champagne glasses to their revolvers and back again.

The colonel repeated his question and added, "Was this a slight to the German language?"

Gurameto shook his head but his explanation was confused. It had nothing to with German. He loved Latin and always had done. He had spoken in Latin impulsively, without thinking. They had spoken Latin in their student days, to tell each other secrets.

The colonel thought for a moment, and sipped his champagne. "You asked me to free the hostages," he said quietly. "Tell me why!"

"They're innocent," the doctor replied. "No other reason."

As they sat at the dinner table, outside in the darkness German soldiers were knocking on the doors of the houses of Gjirokastër.

The doctor asked how the hostages were being selected. Was their fate written on their faces?

The colonel replied that every tenth house was being chosen, as in all reprisals. "Dr Gurameto, you want justice as much as I do. Listen to me! Hand over whoever fired on my advance party and I will release the hostages. On the spot. I give you my word. I give you my word of honour, according to the Code of Lekë Dukagjini."

Gurameto did not reply.

"That's my bargain with the city. This offer is on the table."

Still Dr Gurameto did not speak and the colonel leaned over, his face close to the doctor's. "If the city won't hand them over, give them to me yourself."

The doctor said nothing.

"Gurameto, my brother," the colonel said more gently. "I don't want to spill Albanian blood. I came as a guest, with promises and gifts, but you fired on me." His voice was once again disconsolate, broken.

"Give me those damned names," said the colonel, now almost pleading. "Give them to me and the hostages are yours, instantly."

Gurameto shook his head in refusal, but diffidently. "I can't," he said. "I couldn't even if I wanted to. I don't know who they are. I don't know their names, because they don't have any."

"Now you're playing games with me."

"I'm not joking, Fritz. They don't have names, only nicknames."

One of the officers, apparently belonging to the Gestapo, nodded.

The colonel raised his hands to his head and the doctor drew close to his ear, like at the beginning of the dinner, when they had teased each other about their confidences at the Widow Martha's Tavern.

The colonel listened and then said very softly, "Gurameto, you know some deep mysteries that nobody else does."

Dr Gurameto's reply was a startling one. "So much the worse for you. Free the hostages!"

"I can't." Now it was the colonel's turn to say this.

"Yes you can," said Gurameto. "You know you can."

"If you can't give me their names, at least give me their nicknames," the colonel said in a broken voice.

The guests listened to this crazy conversation, understanding nothing and unable to tell any longer who was giving orders to whom. It was as if the two men were caught in a trap from which they could not escape. Big Dr Gurameto was totally different from what they had thought. Now nobody would be surprised to see him the next governor of Albania, or even Greater Albania, just as had been predicted on the city square. His demeanour suited the part. It would not be unexpected to hear the doctor addressed as "Your Excellency".

What Fritz von Schwabe said was not far short.

"I'll give you seven hostages," he announced in an exhausted voice.

CHAPTER FIVE

At this moment it became clear that there were two currents of events, one inside Big Dr Gurameto's house and one outside in the city. So far separate, these currents now swirled together as if in a vortex of delirium and as they merged they swelled, dissolved, and altered their shape, no longer appearing in their true form.

Yet, one piece of news remained constant: the hostages really were being freed.

Like shadows they crept away from the city square and disappeared in the streets and lanes, where the house-gates had long been left open for them.

Low voices were heard everywhere. "Be careful, don't shout, don't make a noise. No celebrations. Who knows what's happening. They might change their minds and take them back."

The city recalled other long-forgotten tales of hostages. Everyone had their own style of hostage-taking. The Ottoman Turks had one way and Mussolini's troops another, while the Italians did it differently to Albanian brigands, who in turn were not like Macedonian brigands, nor the nomadic Roma. The same was true of governors: the pasha of Janina had been as impetuous as the pasha of Berat had been unhurried and calculating, though that had not prevented the latter from sending back a hostage's head on a dish when the deadline for his ransom expired.

All these memories inevitably prompted a further question. What had the Germans gained in exchange for their release? This was the crux in any hostage story. Give me back my kidnapped wife, and I'll free your prisoner. You want the hostages? Hand over the gold, the murderer, the carpets, the men who fired on the advance party!

The Germans' demand was after all in plain black and white on the posters stuck everywhere: give us the terrorists' names and we'll hand back the hostages!

Some details of the haggling over names in Gurameto's house filtered through.

"We know from Herr Marx that communists have no fatherland, but this is the first time we've heard of them having no names, here on our first evening in Albania!"

And so the conversation turned to nicknames, which seemed so much the fashion in this city. You could be quietly drinking coffee with someone who would suddenly throw you a conspiratorial glance and turn your blood cold by announcing, "Listen, so far I've been called Çelo Nallbani, but you should know that from now on my name is 'Wolf'. Or 'North Pole'." The history of the nicknames did not reach as far back as the stories of hostages but was just as colourful. Some nicknames were easy to interpret and bore a kind of meaning, like "Comrade Lightning" or "The Fist" but others were incomprehensible: "Blah-blah", "Vitamin C" or "Mandolinist".

The Germans must have gained something during the course of their conversation but nobody knew if they had indeed extracted names or had been palmed off with nicknames. Some thought that they might have been sold a mixture of names and nicknames, just as wheat is sometimes bought with chaff.

However the matter was threshed out, there was no avoiding the truly central question: quite apart from the matter of names and nicknames, did this ploy of Big Dr Gurameto's represent treason or not?

Everybody knew that the two sides in this debate would never agree in a thousand years and would both be at odds with a third group of more cautious people, of whom there are always plenty, who took the view that it was hard for the uninitiated to judge those with inside knowledge, or for insiders to judge outsiders and so on. Then they would lose the thread again until a voice piped up, "So what's really going on in there?"

The scene was imagined in two ways. In one, a merry and indeed tipsy Dr Gurameto, at ease in this world of pseudonyms, held a glass of champagne. The alternative version also included Gurameto but this time grim-faced, dramatically handcuffed and with a revolver at his head. Meanwhile the other Dr Gurameto, the little one, was lying low, trembling like a mouse.

Another handful of hostages was released and they too scattered like ghosts. Again whispers went round. "No celebrations, don't make a sound, don't rejoice too soon!" Inevitably people started totting up how many had been freed and how many remained. With astonishing mental agility they calculated the number of hostages that might be released in exchange for one name and how many for a nickname. Of course nicknames were a weak currency compared to real names, rather like ordinary francs compared to gold francs.

When the third and largest batch of hostages was released all at once, most people were of the opinion that either the Germans really had lost their wits, or Dr Gurameto's treason had gone beyond all bounds. Meanwhile the latter's admirers, though fewer in number, were so fervent that they claimed not only that Dr Gurameto was the greatest liberator of hostages in history but that in the course of the dinner his appointment as governor of Albania had arrived directly from Berlin. Only this, and not treachery, could explain the miracle that was taking place. These admirers asserted that there might be some truth in the image of a revolver against a head, but it would be the other way round, with Dr Gurameto holding a gun to the colonel's head as he issued the order, "Fritz, release the hostages!"

But ancient scripture warns against rejoicing too soon and just as the hope blossomed that the last of the hostages would be freed before midnight, it was cut down as if by the stroke of a knife. A curt, cold order was issued at the gate of the house from which the music of the gramophone boomed. "Stop! Halt!" the Germans said. "We've done enough for this city. German magnanimity, the *Nibelungenlied*, Beethoven and so forth has its limits, and so does mercy. We have never before done so much for anyone! Enough!"

The Albanians looked for the reason for the Germans' sudden change of heart among their own past sins. These included their abductions of women (it was believed that each time this happened, a spring ran dry); their periodic incursions into Greece, with all the drums and dudgeon of war, which left only grief and ashes behind. The sacking of the city of Voskopojë, although it happened so long ago, had to be counted among these sins. Finally there were the imperial judges, in whose strongboxes, alongside their silver watch chains, lay ancient court judgments with terrible sentences.

These were their visible sins, startling and gross, but more corrosive than these were their secret, inward falls from grace. The white fancywork, lace and drapery of the old houses sometimes, instead of inspiring admiration, made your flesh creep: it was hard to forget all those memories of incest, dishonoured brides and old people smothered under the awnings of the great verandas.

All these things were recalled to mind but quickly dismissed, until the real snag was hit upon: Jakoel the Jew. Had they really not known this all along or had they pretended that by banishing him from their minds he would be lost in the crowd?

Nothing suggested that the Germans were aware that a special fish had been netted in their catch of hostages, but one could still imagine the tense conversation between Big Dr Gurameto and Fritz von Schwabe on that night across the dinner table.

"Dr Gurameto, you've broken your word. There is a Jew here."

"A Jew? So what?"

"So what? You know I can't release Jews."

"Jews, Albanians, it's all the same."

"It's not the same, Gurameto, not at all."

"Albanians do not betray their guests. You know that, Fritz. This Jew is a guest in our city. We can't hand over a guest."

"Because the *Kanun of Lekë Dukagjini* forbids it?"

"I told you this long ago in the tavern. It's been our law for a thousand years."

The colonel paused doubtfully then shook his head. "In that case Lekë Dukagjini is an enemy of the Reich. I will release them all, but not the Jew."

"No."

"Yes."

"We talked about it in the tavern," said Gurameto in a muffled voice. "But if you're not the same man as then . . ."

These words struck more terror in the colonel than a bolt of lightning.

"Dr Gurameto, do you think I'm not the same man?"

The two stared at each other with cold determination.

"I don't doubt it," said Gurameto wearily. "You are the same man as you were then."

Fritz von Schwabe breathed more easily.

Time was passing.

In the darkness, on the city square, the forty remaining hostages shivered in the cold. Among them, the Jew Jakoel felt the cold most of all. He was on the brink of telling the others to hand him in to save themselves, but his lips would not form the words. All around him was silence and calm. For the first time in many years the nationalists, royalists and communists, who had been at odds over everything else for years, were of the same mind concerning this Jew. Jakoel wanted to weep but the tears would not come.

The discussion in Dr Gurameto's house petered out. Only the gramophone continued its din. The guests looked first at the colonel and then at the doctor, not understanding what was happening. It was as if a dense fog had descended. The rumour was that a second order had just arrived from Berlin, annulling Big Dr Gurameto's appointment as governor and restoring his powers to Fritz von Schwabe.

The colonel himself stood up to change the gramophone record. He put on Schubert's "Death and the Maiden" and everybody realised there was no more hope. And so they sat for a long time, waiting for the rattle of machine guns.

The first cocks crew. A superstition claimed that they drove away ghosts.

The doctor and the colonel muttered to each other in private for a long time and again the situation changed. Nobody explained why. Colonel Fritz von Schwabe, bearer of the Iron Cross, took a deep breath and ordered the hostages to be freed. Not just some, but all of them.

The tension relaxed and it was as if the dinner were starting again. Dr Gurameto's sweet-natured daughter, her chestnut hair combed in the latest fashion, carried in a tray with glasses to celebrate the agreement. All the guests had seen how beautiful she was, even if they had pretended to take no notice. One after another they had fallen in love with her, passionately, as war-weary men do. And she had fallen in love with them. Faced for the first time with such a dense crowd of dangerous masculinity, all men of chivalry, intimate with death, she had fallen suddenly, tremulously in love with them, as if here in this room the men would fill the great emptiness of the future. Her hands trembled as she passed round the drinks to the colonel, then to her father, her mother and to the others in turn and finally, with a slight hesitation, to her fiancé.

They emptied their glasses and the shouts of "Zum Wohl!" mingled with the music of the gramophone as the cocks crew a second time. With soft steps the girl left the drawing room before the exhausted men collapsed on the sofas and on the carpet itself, drifting into a deep sleep.

The girl was woken by the first morning light. For a moment, she could not tell what time it was or why she was lying fully clothed on the bed in her parents' room.

"Oh God, what have I done!" she said in terror, holding her brow.

The house was silent. Her feet carried her involuntarily to the great drawing room, from which a rasping sound came, like the final struggle of a man who finds it hard to die.

She saw them stretched out where they had fallen, arms outspread and mouths gaping, her father, fiancé and mother, in whose lap an officer had laid his head; and then the colonel, his face still masked, and the others, frozen, white, like sculptures.

She turned towards the gramophone. The needle was

stuck, causing the rasping noise. The icy thought ran through her that nobody else could be blamed for the poisoning but herself, the sole person left alive.

CHAPTER SIX

After this unforgettable mid-September night the sun rose, for the first time unobserved by anyone in the stone city. Everybody was still asleep, exhausted by the night's events.

Their waking would become a whole story in itself, to be told in the course of many days and over many cups of coffee. "Where are we?" they asked, as they awoke to find themselves on verandas, in linen cupboards, stretched on the rafters of attics or, as in most cases, on the staircases and in the cellars where sleep had overtaken them. They struggled to work out, if not what time it was, at least the day or the month.

The most difficult question: "What happened?" came last. A thick veil had fallen between them and their memories of events. Behind this veil the story could be discerned dimly, as if it were scared to emerge.

The music of a gramophone was the first thing that seeped through. Then, slowly, and with great effort, people recalled the nightmare of the hostages. The fact that eighty people had lived through the horror of this experience, minute by minute, should have left no room for speculation or error but the hostages did not all tell the same story. Some did not want to admit that they had been hostages, perhaps fearing that in a second wave of arrests they would be told, "You, sir. This is the second time we've arrested you." Other people who had not been hostages were thirsty for fame. They claimed that they had been present facing the machine guns on the city square and were so persuasive that they were believed more readily than genuine hostages.

This confusion added to the general mystery surrounding the events of the day. Out of force of habit these were called "unforgettable", although so many deserved to be forgotten. They were recalled to mind one by one but more and more tentatively. What about the partisan ambush at the entrance to the city? God knows what really happened there. There were no eyewitness accounts and there was no physical evidence apart from two black skid marks on the asphalt, where it was thought the German motorcycles had turned back.

Probably there really had been an ambush, which the communists called heroic and the nationalists considered a provocation, but it was equally plausible that the whole incident had been invented by the Germans to justify their tactics of terror.

The ambush could be interpreted to the credit of all three parties, but the same could hardly be said of the incident of the white sheet, which was taken as a sign of surrender to the Germans. It was easy to call it a mirage but seen by whom, the inhabitants of the city or the German Army?

Obviously Gurameto's famous dinner was the biggest mystery of all. It had started as Big Dr Gurameto's fairy-tale reunion with his German college friend. But the rest went beyond any fairy tale. The invitation to dinner, the gradual release of the hostages, not to mention the climax at dawn in the Gurameto house, the motionless Germans laid out in deathly sleep in the drawing room and the doctor's daughter, thinking she had poisoned them, and then the Germans slowly stirring, resurrected as if at Easter time, not one Christ but a whole cohort of Christs. This was not just a disgrace to the house but a blasphemous parody.

All these events might have been accepted as imaginary had it not been for one detail: the music of the gramophone. This music had blared all night and everyone had heard it. It might have been taken for a crazy whim on the part of Gurameto, of a kind familiar to the city, where the more respected its citizens were, the more impulsive they were likely to be in their caprices. And yet it was hardly likely that Dr Gurameto would get it into his head on the night of the German invasion to play his gramophone in hermit-like seclusion.

Unable to account for this extraordinary hiatus, people inevitably suggested the influence of some *force majeure*, like the Double Night. It was as if, after lying in wait for a thousand years, this monster had finally descended to enfold forty or more hours in its arms, seizing a whole day like a wolf snatching a sheep, and had vanished again into the infinite depths of time.

But as people's heads cleared, so their eyes regained their proper vision. On either side of the iron gates in the city square hung two long flags with the swastika in their centre. Above them was a huge banner in both Albanian and German, appealing for recruits to the newly founded Albanian gendarmerie. A long queue of elderly men had formed by the side entrance before dawn. The German sentries stared in astonishment at their strange gowns and cloaks to which were pinned unheard-of insignia and stripes. These were the old judges of the former empire, who hoped to find employment. From the folds of their robes peered their letters of appointment and copies of their judgments and rulings with their seals and signatures, from all their different postings throughout the boundless Ottoman dominions.

The Albanian interpreter in the ground-floor office found it hard to render into German their records of service, in which the old men placed so many hopes. These described the variety of sentences they had handed down, not just usual ones like beheading and hanging but more sophisticated ones like skinning and dismemberment alive, drowning in vats of boiling water or tepid water in a tank with two snakes. There were other forms of drowning (one involving a monkey) and two ways of being buried alive: one with the legs and part of the trunk under the earth and the head and chest above, and one the other way round. At this point the German officer interrupted the Albanian interpreter with a tactful expression of thanks, adding that Germany had its own forms of punishment and the Third Reich was not a Mongol empire, an expression that struck the old men as "not in very good taste".

Meanwhile the city's newspaper *Demokratia* had reappeared, full of news from the capital. Albania, following its liberation by the Third Reich, had cast off the hated Italian yoke and had been declared a sovereign state. A government had been formed headed not by the famous Mehdi Frashëri, as hoped, but by a respected gentleman named Biçaku. Indeed, a Regency Council had been set up with four members, one for each religious community, evidently in expectation of the return of King Zog I. In even larger type came news of the unification of Kosovo and Çamëria with Albania and a headline announcing the restoration of the ancient Albanian flag: the real standard of Skanderbeg was to be used again, with the black eagle and without the lictor's fasces, which were a bitter memory of Italy.

Other reports described the spread of Albanian-language schools in Kosovo, supported by research that demonstrated the superiority of Albanian to most other Balkan languages and sometimes the superiority of the Albanian race itself.

When read to the accompaniment of the rousing strains of the hurriedly assembled municipal band, which played every day, the news seemed easy to believe. But when dusk fell and the communists scattered their leaflets, it all became more questionable. The leaflets urged the people not to trust the occupiers, who were merely throwing dust in the Albanians' eyes with their talk of Kosovo and Çamëria and their flattery of the Albanian race. The communists claimed that the nationalists and royalists were preparing to do a deal with the Germans. The leaflets ended with the words "Now or never!" Both the communists and the nationalists made use of this phrase. In fact it had been current for more than a century, which made it hard to work out when "now" and especially "never" might be.

A fraction of this would have given anyone sleepless nights but it was particularly those citizens who hated anarchy and yearned for law and order who made their way to the city square each morning with bloodshot eyes, to sit in the cafés and read the newspapers as the music played.

Besides the news, the government announcements and the music, there was something else that made everyone think back to peacetime with a pang of nostalgia. Each morning the two famous surgeons, Big Dr Gurameto and Little Dr Gurameto, walked to the city hospital, just as in the time of the Albanian monarchy and in the time of the triple Italian-Albanian-African empire. Now, under what some people were calling Teutonic Albania, there was a new hospital set up in the house of Remzi Kadare, the same house that its owner had lost at cards three months before.

The general conviction was that as long as these two doctors remained (with all their ups and downs, gramophones and dinners and non-dinners), the city was still intact.

In fact, many people were doing their best to push the city over the edge. On some days it seemed to come close to the brink, only to be saved at the last moment.

With the arrival of winter it became clear that there was no brink. The communists' calls for war and the nationalists' for peace mingled like two opposing winds to create a kind of in-between state that was neither one nor the other.

Trouble, when it appeared, took the form of a moral scandal of an unprecedented nature. The newspaper *Demokratia* said that it was the only case of its kind involving two men on the entire war-torn continent of Europe. A municipal employee Bufe Hasani was caught in flagrante in the city hall basement, to his shame, with a German!

No earthquake could have shaken the city more. After their initial blush of shame, people's first thought was again of being blown up. This would no doubt be the inevitable reprisal, but this time, a merited one. Things had gone too far! Everybody said so. All the city's inhabitants knew how cautiously, almost bashfully, the German soldiers behaved towards the local women: they were believed to be under orders not to trifle with the Albanians' lofty sense of propriety. But the city, not satisfied with this courtesy, and as if on purpose to hold it up to ridicule, had now provoked a different lust and violated the honour of a blond-haired German lad, barely eighteen, as pale as a young girl. Gjirokastër could no longer protest at being blown up. It was the very least it deserved.

As can be imagined many people turned to Big Dr Gurameto for assistance, but he raised his hands helplessly. "This time I'm not interfering!"

He added that if it had been a matter of a woman, he would have spoken to Fritz von Schwabe, but this sort of business was not something he dealt with.

Some people saw no reason to tear their hair and cry "Shame!", arguing that the occurrence was the logical consequence of a policy that was neither war nor peace. If you wanted this kind of thing, that is, war and peace at the same time and a city confused, there it was in the city hall basement. They said this wasn't the first time Albanians had got up to such tricks. Whenever an Albanian sees that one sword is no good, he'll sheathe it and draw another one.

In fact, from a more balanced point of view, the case of Bufe Hasani was merely a symptom. Like Big Dr Gurameto's dinner, the incident in the cellar could be looked at in two ways. Indeed it was not just an Albanian phenomenon but had global implications. It recalled Hitler's humili-ation of the British in the Munich agreement. Mentioning

Bufe Hasani and Neville Chamberlain in the same breath prompted grimaces, but the matter was essentially the same.

Feelings of fear and shame floated in the air; whenever fear rose, shame sank and vice versa.

Meanwhile there were other developments, some visible and others secret. Bufe Hasani's two sons put together a bomb designed to kill their degenerate father but then set it aside, expecting a proper solution to their problem when the city was blown up. At this moment the prime minister of the newly formed government, Mehdi Frashëri, arrived in the city to deal with the issue. What a pity that the first duty of this scion of the most famous of all Albanian families, whose arrival was so eagerly awaited, was to tackle such a nasty business.

He arrived and left again at night, without ceremony, with no dinner or gramophone, as was to be expected with this kind of case in hand. But his visit still brought reassurance.

Comforting news for the nationalists also came from the Albanians' two capital cities, Tirana and Prishtina. There was a rumour that the Albanian communist leader had been captured and punished: after his eyes were gouged out, he had been forced to practise his family's traditional profession of washing corpses in the Et'hem Bey Mosque in Tirana.

Bufe Hasani's exploit was gradually forgotten, except when little children unexpectedly asked, "Mummy, what did Bufe Hasani do with that German uncle in the cellar of the city hall?"

The surest sign of restored order was of course the renewed attention paid to the two doctors, or rather the rise and fall of their relative reputations. The doctors had become as used to this as to sunrise and sunset and it seemed too late to tempt them to a new challenge. As ever, their relative positions were measured with reference to the international situation, and the prospects were not looking good for the Germans. At first sight this suggested that Big Dr Gurameto would fall behind. However, his standing was calculated only relative to Little Dr Gurameto's, and Italy was the last country likely to benefit from Germany's weakness, so it seemed that Little Dr Gurameto would be the loser again.

The two now worked together in the new surgical ward that was housed on the first floor of the great mansion of the Kadare family. Surely peace would prevail here at least, where patients spent their last days, facing the prospect of death. But the opposite was the case. For anybody hankering to see pure civil war, the ward of the two Gurametos was the place to go, or so the correspondent of the local paper reported. Bloody bandages, screams, vituperation, horror. The sick seemed afraid only of dying before they had vented their political hatreds. This was the sole explanation for the continual uproar, the insults and the moans and shouts of "traitor to your country!" They would come to blows with medicine bottles, there were assaults with syringes and even an amputated arm that one patient had asked to be left beside him, protesting he would miss it, but really to keep it within reach if things came to a fight.

According to the journalist the two Gurametos could hardly keep this bedlam under control, although many also formed the impression that the two doctors were merely waiting for the ward to calm down before attacking each other with scalpels and bloody forceps.

As evening fell, another man was listening carefully to the tumult from the upper floor. The unhinged Remzi Kadare, the former owner of the house, huddled in army blankets, added his own expletives to the bedlam above. "You tart! You whore!" he shouted, addressing the house that had been his own home before he lost it at poker. "That's what the place deserves," he roared. "Drip blood and gall! I knew you weren't to be trusted. I was right to take a chance with you! I risked you and lost you, you bitch!"

The night gradually grew colder and he wrapped himself more tightly in the blankets. Burying his head in them, he sang to himself.

I saw a nightmare, mother, the worst of all my dreams
Our big house was a hospital, full of groans and screams.

I woke from sleep, dear mother, and wept at dawn of
   day
I thought I'll burn it down, or gamble it away.

And so I did, dear mother, and I'm a wretched knave
My wife has gone to Janina, and you are in your grave.

Remzi was my first name, my surname Kadare
You should have fed me poison when at your breast
   I lay.

The weeks passed quickly. Winter held the city under its stern rule. But this meant little to the mind of Vehip Qorri. "Blind Vehip" had been a rhymester since the previous century, before there were newspapers. As his nickname indicated, he had been blind since birth but even though he had never seen the world, he described it accurately in verses that were full of dates and the names of people and streets. He composed some of his rhymes to order and for a small fee, to mark occasions of every kind such as birthdays or the award of decorations, to advertise barber shops, or announce changes of address and opening hours. He produced others to publicise court verdicts, quarrels, scandals, municipal notices, riding accidents, the imposition of fines, cases of intoxication, the downfall of governments, currency devaluations and the like. People who enjoyed rhymes would stop at the street corner where he had his pitch, ask for verses about X or Y and pay him or not, according to how they liked the result.

Sometimes his customers, for one reason or another (when faced with threats for instance, or when an engagement that the rhyme celebrated was broken off) asked him to remove a verse from his repertoire, again for a fee. This would cost more than the original composition.

That was Blind Vehip's daily routine. Occasionally, but very rarely, he would take it into his head to compose a rhyme without a commission, "from the heart", as he put it. His usual rhymes were topical but his verses "from the heart" were obscure and elusive.

At the end of April he produced a verse about Big Dr Gurameto, perhaps his grimmest yet.

> Gurameto, the mortal sinner
> Met the devil one day on the street,
> Who told him to host a great dinner
> With champagne and good things to eat.

His listeners did not say what they thought of this verse. At first they merely frowned, turned their backs and walked slowly away. Gurameto no doubt understood the rhyme completely but he was totally aloof to anything that happened on the street and took no notice. Then the audience began to grow steadily at Blind Vehip's usual spot at the crossroads of Varosh Street and the road to the *lycée*. Dr Gurameto passed here regularly on his way to the hospital but never turned his head.

Two weeks later, Blind Vehip, perhaps smarting at the snub or maybe simply on a whim, produced a new version of his rhyme. Now the words made your flesh creep.

> What was the doctor's design,
> Asking the corse to dine?

The archaic word "corse" that old people still used to refer to the dead made it seem more frightening; perhaps this was what led Big Dr Gurameto to swallow his pride and, early one evening, stop in front of old Vehip. He waved a couple of idlers away with his hand. "What have you got against me?" he said.

The blind man recognised his voice and shrugged his shoulders. "Nothing. What could I ever have against you? Just look at yourself, compared to me."

"You're lying. You've got it in for me. But you won't tell me why."

The blind man paused for a moment, and then said curtly, "No."

Dr Gurameto was famously reticent but his silence was still striking.

"That dinner seems so long ago," he eventually said in a low voice. "I can barely remember it myself. Why bring it up now?"

"I don't know."

Gurameto turned his head to make sure no one was listening. "Do you really believe that I invited the dead to dinner that night?"

"I don't know what to say," the blind man replied.

Gurameto stared at him fixedly. "Vehip," he said. "I want to ask you something, as a doctor. Do you remember when you lost your sight?"

"No," the blind man said. "I was born like this."

"I see. So you've never seen living people."

"Neither the living, nor the dead," said Vehip.

"I see," repeated Dr Gurameto.

"That comes as a surprise to you, I can tell," the blind man said. "You're surprised that I've never seen the living, but still more surprised I've never seen the dead."

"That's true," said Gurameto. "Blindness is close to death. I won't interfere with you. I'm not threatening you and I won't promise anything. Make whatever rhymes you like."

As he walked away, he heard the blind man's voice behind him. "Long live the doctor!"

PART TWO

1944

CHAPTER SEVEN

The German Army retreated from Greece and Albania at the same time. It looked like a routine redeployment of troops. An unending column of vehicles rumbled all night along the asphalted highway. Daybreak came feebly, ash-grey. A fine rain turned to sleet, making the windows of the houses opaque. It seemed only natural for the city to show no interest in this great historical event.

The regiment housed in the Grihot barracks joined the long convoy and the troops from inside the city itself followed them. There were neither farewells nor appeals to the people to cover the withdrawal with rearguard attacks against the encroaching forces of communism. The old threats to blow up the city now seemed stale and empty.

The Germans lowered the swastika flag and left the national flag with the lonely eagle in the centre. With no sign of pride or shame and no reaction to the city's indifference, the Germans climbed into their vehicles and set off to find new terrain.

A NEW ORDER

Just before noon the communist partisans entered the city

from not one but three different directions. They stared at the great houses of Gjirokastër with awe and smiled hesitantly, uncertain where to put the welcoming flowers the citizens threw at them.

The mules could barely climb the steep lanes and looked wearier than the fighters themselves. Most were laden with mortar barrels and crates of ammunition, yet the partisans led them by the halter as if they were carrying grain or cheeses wrapped in cloth.

The young women among them attracted particular attention. They wore their hair in all kinds of styles, plaited, cropped, with long tresses or fashionable fringes. There had been contradictory rumours about them: either they were "Red virgins" who would kill at the slightest affront or they were wild about men.

The scene looked so peaceful, yet the city's fears of what the partisans might do turned out to be well-founded. The first knocks at the gates of houses were followed by the wails of women and screams. "He's innocent." "Traitor! Get away, bitches." "No!" And then the stutter of gunfire. "Territorials", as the local communists were called, helped the patrols to carry out arrests of prominent nationalists.

Just after noon, at the precise moment when the flag was hoisted over the city hall, the partisans arrived at the hospital to arrest Big Dr Gurameto. He was handcuffed while in his surgical gown, halfway through an operation, before the partisans realised he should be allowed to wash his bloody hands. But the doctor merely said, "Why should I bother?" thinking he would be shot at once. He walked unsteadily and glanced instinctively at the flag above the city hall, which was now different in a slight but unexpected way.

"Get a move on!" said a partisan as Gurameto stumbled. The doctor looked down at his handcuffs, as if to protest that he was not used to managing in these things, but the partisan didn't understand him. "Move!" he said again.

The eagle on the flag still had two heads as before, not three as had been rumoured.

"This way," said the partisan when they reached the crossroads.

"What have I done?" Big Dr Gurameto wanted to ask, but the flag caught his eye again. Instead of a third head, which it was optimistically claimed would symbolise the unity of the communists, royalists and nationalists, a pale star shone above the double-headed eagle. "I see," the doctor thought, staring at the fabric of the flag as if it could answer his question.

Both sides of the street were thronged with idlers and a few musicians carried mandolins. Messengers hurried past. The flag fluttered enigmatically in the wind and gave no answer.

A breathless messenger appeared and ran alongside the patrol for a few paces, struggling to say something.

"Halt," said the patrol leader and stopped first himself. The messenger muttered something into his ear and the patrol leader looked at Dr Gurameto in surprise. Then, taking care not to stain his hands with blood, he removed the doctor's handcuffs.

"Pardon our mistake, doctor," he said quietly.

The territorial, who had been watching the scene with curiosity, whispered to the partisan. The other man nodded. As Gurameto turned to walk away he thought he caught a mention of Little Dr Gurameto's name but he could not be sure.

The doctor walked down the street, looking for a tap to rinse his hands, but he couldn't remember if there was one nearby. He was almost back at the hospital when he recognised the same patrol again, now coming from the opposite direction. In their midst was Little Dr Gurameto, handcuffed as he himself had been a short time ago.

The two doctors inclined their heads towards each other to suggest they could not tell what was happening, when the explanation flashed through Big Dr Gurameto's mind. The territorial, used to the idea that the rise of one entailed the fall of the other, had persuaded the patrol that the release of the big doctor must lead to the arrest of the little one. Gurameto was sure that his colleague would go free too. He entered the hospital, cursing in German.

Little Dr Gurameto was indeed released a short time later. The two doctors embraced as if after a long separation, to the delight of the nurses. But at that moment another patrol, with set faces, appeared at the hospital entrance. The two doctors glanced at each other, wondering what this could mean. Would they be put in handcuffs again? But what the patrol asked was unimaginable. They wanted to arrest two patients as "enemies of the people". Both were fresh from the operating table and one was still under anaesthetic.

The two Gurametos dropped their heads in their hands. "Are you crazy? This man has an open wound, and you want to tie him up!"

"You're the crazy one here," barked the patrol leader. "We have orders, full stop. Do you think you can stop us?"

The nurses joined the doctors in protest but the patrol

would not be deterred. They produced the handcuffs, secured them this time on both doctors and set off for the city hall.

The patrol brought both doctors back to the hospital an hour later. The partisans were a noisy rabble. The two doctors' hands were now free. A grey-haired man who claimed to be an impartial legal expert was trying in vain to calm everyone as they yelled, shouting each other down and brandishing revolvers and syringes under each other's noses. "This is unheard of! This man's at death's door. He has one hand cut off and you're going to shackle the other one. Where's your humanity?"

"You call this humanity?" shouted a partisan. "You let criminals kill and maim and then tuck them up in hospital to save them from the people's courts?"

The grey-haired lawyer negotiated a compromise: the wanted patients would be neither arrested nor released. The nurse in charge remembered there was a room in the hospital's west wing with a grille over the window. Remzi Kadare had left legal instructions that he should be incarcerated here if he lost his mind.

They carried the accused patients there and left a partisan with a rifle and two grenades in his belt to guard the door.

DAY TWO, DAWN

The elderly judges, who were known as "the three hundred", had not exercised their profession for a very long time. That morning they turned up at the door of the city hall, which was now known as the Committee. They brought all their ancient insignia and testimonials, in the conviction that they could still be of service to their country.

The Committee chairman could not conceal a certain satisfaction as he heard them out. His words of thanks at the end of the meeting made it clear that his pleasure was genuine. These three hundred were throwbacks to a vanished era but they had grasped sooner than all Albania's pansy intellectuals that the revolution demanded ruthless violence.

The former judges listened to the talk of a new era and new laws, plainly surprised that such things could exist. Their services were declined but as the old men left, they remarked on how flattered they felt at being turned down so courteously.

DAY MINUS TWO

Besides the arrested patients, three others in the surgical ward had still not come round from their anaesthetic. A kidney patient was the first to surface and was met by a nurse who tried to explain to him that they were now living under a new order. It was not easy for the patient to take this in. As the other inmates woke up, the kidney patient launched into an explanation of what had happened. The others clustered round him as if listening to a fairy tale. The kidney patient said that important events had taken place in the city and in this very ward, but they had been fast asleep and had known nothing about them.

When the kidney patient saw that the others did not seem surprised, he started at the beginning again. All hell had been let loose in the city while they had been absent, as if down a rabbit hole. "The era we were in no longer exists, see? The times have moved on. Hours, days are passing and we are still stuck somewhere – I don't know how to describe it. Out of time. In reverse or minus time."

"I don't understand this," said a patient on crutches. "Say it straight. What's this new time you're talking about?"

"It's called a new order. It's what happens when the system changes. The first day is usually called zero hour. Then the numbering starts, one, two, three and so on. When they gave us the anaesthetic it was, let's say, a certain time on such-and-such a day. We went under, and out of time. But time paid no attention. Time doesn't wait, it goes on, and we were left behind. They've reached day two but we're not even at zero. We're minus. Now do you see it?"

"I see bullshit," said a third patient.

"We have a time deficit," he continued, ignoring him. "We'll have to hurry to catch up to zero, and then we'll see."

"You've got us in a proper muddle," said the appendix case. "Just tell us who's won. In fact, I don't care who it is as long as it's not the communists."

"I think it's them," said the third.

"No!" said the other patient. "Anyone but them!"

"In this new order you mentioned, are you allowed to kill your wife?" asked one patient on crutches. "Like in Yemen for instance."

"What can you be thinking about?"

"I told you what I was thinking about."

"Your wife? I don't think so. But other people . . . perhaps."

★

Of all the expressions involving time, the most common was "the new era".

On some days it seemed that such a thing really had come to pass. Everything appeared bathed in triumphant, dazzling sunlight, as if fresh from the suds of the washtub. But then another morning would dawn, ashen and exhausted, to confirm the view that time is the last thing in this world that is capable of renewal.

Nevertheless, if this "time" never seemed exactly reborn, there was something youthful about it. It was always a little hectic. There were incessant campaigns, one after another. There was a touch of fever especially in the chatter of the activists, who promised and threatened all kinds of things. Down with soil erosion! Glory to the martyrs! Hang the speculators! Forwards with reforestation!

There was no end of meetings. Hoarders of gold were denounced, along with the Corfu Channel incident, the rhymes of Blind Vehip and Nietzsche's idea of the Superman. The rejection of the concept of perpetual motion was for some reason connected to the latter. The idea of "the new era" was always closely associated with "reconstruction". Slogans were painted and songs sung everywhere about the new era, as if she were a bride.

"Work" and "reconstruction" usually meant digging irrigation channels. People got up before dawn, unfurled a banner and marched off in single file to start digging. It turned out later that some of the new ditches didn't raise the level of water but merely diverted it from other channels, or failed to drain away flood waters and actually increased them. When people were punished for this it gradually became clear that the ditches, besides their ostensible function, had a different purpose that was more important.

"Don't stare like that. There's no great mystery here," said a newly arrested engineer to his two cellmates. They were all in prison for sabotaging ditches. "It's the same old story. It goes back to the Babylonians. That's where tyranny began, they say. Either too much water, or too little. Water wanted in one place, but not in another."

Two sensational items of news, about the start of the Cold War and Tito's treachery, seemed to have something to do with the ditches. Other questions, including some of a purely mental nature, however remote they might appear, were also related.

Farewell to wandering thoughts, to whatever crossed your mind – ancient decrees, women's private parts – to any thought either elevated or shameful. It became clearer every day that you had to think about some things a lot and others much less, if at all.

One of the things in the latter class was the famous dinner with the Germans. It was as if it had never happened. In fact anyone mentioning it even in passing was firmly rounded on. "What, you still believe those old tales about the German and the doctor being old school friends and all that blah-blah?" Yet this did not stem the rumours that somewhere, at a secret level you didn't dare think about, the dinner was still being investigated. Indeed, the recently appointed chorus master at the House of Culture was suspected of being one of two undercover investigators. You would never guess the other in a thousand years, although it was generally known that this person had planted the suspicion that there had never been any dinner at all. He claimed that the gramophone had played to an empty room and a secret meeting in the guise of a dinner had taken place somewhere else, in order to leave no evidence behind.

A SEQUENCE OF SEASONS

It was winter. A few weeks before, the Cold War had started. This was no longer the laughing matter it had been at first (Eskimos etcetera), but nor was it as frightening as it later became (silent and as frigid as death). It was something to be worried about, like the Iron Curtain, invented by an English lord.

In order to demonstrate that it was possible to live with these fears, and even cheerfully, the number of festivals increased. Sports days were the favourite: they were cheap and needed no preparation. You gathered a few dozen time-wasters with itchy feet and all it took was a sign reading "Spring Cross-Country" for them to pelt off like lunatics. Along the road others would join in and then they would stop in some square to catch their breath and cheer, "Long live . . . " and just as often "Death to . . . ", for there were as many things that had to live as to die, and the quicker the better.

Almost as frequent were concerts, races, inaugurations and, in particular, award ceremonies. These latter were often of an unusual nature. For instance in the first week of April there were celebrations for Big Dr Gurameto's twelve-thousandth operation.

As one can imagine, the little doctor was not forgotten

although, as a lesser light, he had barely reached his nine-thousandth. That afternoon and evening old memories revived of the time when these two rivals had been the centre of attention. As in the old days, one was weighed against the other. This was a hard task because everybody knew that their relative status still depended primarily on the international situation.

After its defeat in the war Germany had been divided into a bad part and a good part, leaving Big Dr Gurameto roughly neutral. Italy was not as bad as West Germany, but not as good as East Germany, so he and Little Dr Gurameto were more or less quits. In short, they had emerged from the global upheaval fifty–fifty, as the English say.

The wave of affection for Big Dr Gurameto was all the stronger because of the memory of the rivalry between the two doctors, which had become a symbol of a past now recalled, for some reason, with nostalgia.

"Oh, how touching," said Marie Turtulli, one of the city's great ladies. "What sweet memories," she repeated after a moment. "Just like in la Belle Époque."

The rosy aureole surrounding the two doctors was best described in a rhyme by Blind Vehip,

> The Gurametos, doctors both,
> True to the Hippocratic oath.

Yet whispers persisted that the dinner of long ago was the subject of an investigation, still a covert one but now conducted by two independent groups. Its German aspect was lately overshadowed by its supernatural dimension; the dinner was associated mainly with the appearance of a dead man, who, for the purpose of disguise or some other reason, had worn the greatcoat of a German officer and in this shape, spattered with mud, had knocked at Dr Gurameto's door.

DAY FIVE HUNDRED
A SPECTRAL THRONG OF GERMAN SYMPATHISERS

On the five-hundredth day of the new order there appeared a sight that should never have been seen. Beneath the city the first refugees from Çamëria arrived. There was no end to them. The Greeks had accused them of having supported the Germans and expelled them northwards across the border. They all brought evidence of recent atrocities: cradles with knife marks, old people scarred by burns, young wives blackened from the soot of their torched houses. They walked in an endless column under a bitter, pitiless wind.

To their left stood the first city in Albania, of which they had so often dreamed. But they had strict orders, nobody knew from whom, not to enter it. The city loomed above them, as inscrutable as a sphinx, inaccessible and failing to understand why it could not take them in. Who suffered most from this prohibition, the convoy of refugees or the city? To be sure it pained both, as if they had been showered with the debris of some terrible catastrophe. That afternoon the very rafters of Gjirokastër's houses began to groan. The city suffered an agony of conscience. Receiving no mercy themselves, the refugees showed none for anybody else. Old loyalties had lost their meaning. Neither side in this conflict could claim victory, or even sustain their quarrel.

It was scant consolation for the losers, the nationalists and the royalists, to recall how they had cheered for Çamëria and Kosovo: now they guiltily hung their heads. For perhaps it was these cheers that had to be paid for after the German defeat.

Migrations like this were said to be happening everywhere. An evil hour had struck for whole populations, entire peoples uprooted from their homes from the shores of the Baltic to the snowfields of the Caucasus and deep into the distant steppes, supposedly for supporting the Germans.

Other dreadful convoys came to mind. The Jews, three years ago. The Armenians, thirty years before.

The citizens of Gjirokastër watched the scene through binoculars and yearned for an end to these columns from Çamëria, but one convoy seemed to spawn another. It was said that in the Greek-minority villages, at night, people would offer them bread but they would not take it. They had expected that someone else would feed them.

Where were they going? Perhaps north to the olive groves of Vlora. It was rumoured that there the sky had filled with the cruel sound of thunder but something uncanny happened: the lightning rebelled against the laws of nature and refused to fall on these wretches' heads.

CHAPTER EIGHT

THE NEW ORDER CONTINUED

Dawn rose on the asphalted highway and on this bleak day spirits sank even lower. The cold tightened its grip on Gjirokastër. The coal ran out and martyrs were in short supply.

As if to a natural disaster, trucks of food and medicine were hurriedly dispatched from the capital city with inspectors, musical ensembles and delegations of all kinds, some from fraternal countries. One of these, from the Soviet Baltic republics, where something similar had happened, issued a strange communiqué before it returned, stating that the situation in Gjirokastër called for a more radical approach. In the city there were still eleven former vezirs and pashas of the Ottoman Empire, four former overseers of the sultan's harem, three former deputy managers of Italian-Albanian banks, fifteen ex-prefects of various regimes, two professional stranglers of heirs apparent, a street called "Lunatics' Lane" and two high-class courtesans, not to mention the famous three hundred former judges and more than six hundred cases of insanity: a lot for a medieval city now striving to become a communist one.

The Baltic delegation's communiqué made plain that what

was required was an upsurge of renewal, what the newspapers called "new blood". Very soon this became a flood. Every day enthusiastic young volunteers arrived from central Albania: overfulfillers of already overfulfilled plans, on the Soviet model, some singing the song "Pickaxe in one hand, rifle in the other", or not just singing about these implements but actually carrying them; informers on saboteurs of ill-planned drainage ditches; informers on fastidious ladies who rarely left their homes in a demonstration of disdain for the new order; activists who only looked forward to the future and others that did so mainly but not exclusively, and occasionally glanced back; sculptors of busts of martyrs; self-sacrificing zealots keen to join the latter in their graves, if nature permitted; opponents of the ideological enemies known as "the three 'no's" (imperialism, Zionism and Coca-Cola) and others of the seven 'no's; nutcases obsessed with cultivating friendship with other nations and others entranced by the notion of hostility. In short, a perfect frenzy that made everyone weep.

Just when everything seemed on track again, a secret report drawn up by an even more secret delegation from the capital announced bluntly that the rate of progress was still not satisfactory. The ditches, however unnecessary, were being dug too slowly. The former vezirs, hangovers from the time of the sultan, were not dying fast enough. Except for the two high-class courtesans, who had "distanced themselves from their bourgeois past" and joined the new order out of inner conviction, the other remnants of the old order were stubbornly clinging on.

A song was heard in the streets, of the anonymous kind that appeared in Gjirokastër. It spread everywhere and seemed to confirm the secret report. Its words were sad, and its melody even more plangent.

> Lena lies sick in a hospital bed.
> In the lonely ward, her hopes are dead.

The authorities did all they could to prevent people singing it, but in vain.

Nobody had ever imagined that a song about a hospital could become the reason for another dramatic development in the city: the campaign against its ladies. It all started at a meeting at which a senior cultural official complained that people were still singing songs of what might be called a private nature, about how you've forgotten me but I'll never forget you, you didn't visit me in hospital, I couldn't get rid of my cough and twaddle of this sort. The city's leaders suggested commissioning local musicians to compose two or three songs for the new era, which still had a bit of feeling in them. The Party chairman butted in. "Come out with it – you mean about being ill." Without more ado he phoned the two doctors, Big and Little Gurameto, to demand the names of the singing patients.

At first the doctors were at a loss how to respond. Big Dr Gurameto replied that they were surgeons and their patients either recovered or went straight to their graves and had no time for sighing and groaning, so it would be better to ask other doctors who dealt with protracted illnesses such as typhus and especially tuberculosis.

Meanwhile, taking advantage of the turbulent times, the Romany guard at the Hygiene Institute known as "Dan the TB Man" produced a song in memory of his girlfriend, who had been run over that April by the night-soil cart.

> I'm the gypsy of the institute
> In an awful plight
> Since the girl I loved
> Fell under a load of shite.

The cultural officials chuckled but soon wiped the smiles from their faces. At their next meeting, which turned out to be fatal for them all, they agreed that private feelings involved not only disease and filth, but also nobler sentiments. Unaware of how dearly he would pay for this later, the head of culture recalled an old women's song.

> Sing, nightingale, sing tonight
> In our garden of delight.
> In your wings of song enfold us,
> If we slumber wake us,
> From all intrusion guard us
> From all detection hide us.

The exclamations of how lovely, how delicate, what sensitivity, prompted the head of culture, as if with the devil at his elbow, to recollect another song describing the same women, this time from the men's point of view.

> Happy lads who woo them, happy lads
>   who love them
> Happy lads who count them theirs . . .

Retribution came swiftly at an emergency meeting of the Party Committee before the week was out. The meeting denounced decadent trends in the city, nostalgia for the overthrown feudal-bourgeois order and the cult of declassed ladies, whose degraded songs were cunningly described simply as "women's songs" instead of "songs of the elite", as our literary critics have classified them.

Angry voices were raised. "Who's at the bottom of this?" The head of culture fainted twice. Towards midnight the Party chairman made a start on his closing speech with a quotation from Lenin. "Your most dangerous enemy is the one you forget." He spared no one, not even himself. "Our enemies have caught us napping. Decadence, thrown out the front door, has returned through the back window." Before properly settling accounts with the notions of Nietzsche, perpetual motion and other perversities, the city was confronted with this virulent plague: its ladies. It was no coincidence that this was happening at a time of renewed tension with Greece and that the US Sixth Fleet had been patrolling the Mediterranean for days. "We will punish the culprits without mercy. Brace yourself for the worst."

Shortly after the meeting ended, towards two in the morning, the head of culture shot himself.

THE CITY CONFRONTS ITS LADIES

The bullet that claimed the life of the head of culture was also in a way the first shot in a war between the city's new authorities and its ladies. For those in the know it was obvious that the head of culture had died a victim of his own nostalgia for the ladies but, for reasons that remained unknown, this detail was quickly concealed and he was portrayed as their opponent, indeed a sort of first martyr in this new battle.

The meetings to denounce the ladies, unlike the usual ones, were conducted not only without cheering or music but with a sombre, even academic tinge that seemed appropriate to their subject. This was especially true of the opening presentation entrusted to the elderly antiquarian Xixo Gavo, which, despite its imposing title "A Thousand Years of Ladies", was merely a recitation of an interminable list of the city's ladies from 1361 until the previous week. Nobody in the audience understood what it was for but this did not prevent them from applauding the old historian when the list, and with it his speech, came to an end.

The other contributions more or less compensated for the shortcomings of the opening speech. One of them, "Ladies Under Communism", not only surveyed, as the title suggested, the fate of ladies everywhere in the communist camp, from Budapest to the former St Petersburg, Bratislava and even Shanghai, but explained why the ladies of Gjirokastër occupied a special position in this vast field.

This was also the most obscure part of the talk, which each listener interpreted in his or her own way. According to the speaker, being a lady in this city, or occupying "lady status" did not depend so much on the title and property of a husband. Rather, it was something to do with large houses. It was no coincidence that a foreign architect had called these houses "ladies in stone". According to him, inside these great houses no doubt constructed by deranged craftsmen, under their gingerbread ceilings and behind the pitiless glare of their windowpanes, there took place a mysterious and sophisticated process, like a retreat into a moonlit distance, which was the first symptom of the formation of a lady. These ladies were imagined as impossibly pale, their breasts and waists dazzlingly white, with a dark enigma hidden under silk that made the senses reel.

A sigh of relief followed the conclusion of the talk.

The next paper was easier to comprehend because it dealt with the events that had led to the death of the poor cultural official and also took a clear political position. From the very start the speaker did not hide his hostility to the ladies. He considered their songs, which many people recalled with tenderness, to be indubitably decadent. As for their coffee ritual, evoked in the words, "The coffee service arrives/Like a decree from the sultan", this might be thought to describe a custom of aristocratic dignity, and even inspire admiration. But it struck this expert, who had been nurtured at the bosom of the people, merely as evidence that the ladies of the city were not just discriminating aristocrats, but women of power. Intoxicated by his own eloquence, the speaker lifted his head high to announce that these women had tyrannised the city for years.

An intervention by the chairman asking for this contribution to be cut short only spurred on the speaker. He did not stop but screeched that these ladies not only wielded power but were the city's hidden face, its soul, its exact reflection. This, he claimed, was the explanation of the insane fantasies that flourished in this city, fictions about dinners for the dead and the like.

There was no doubt that the ladies were being targeted and it was obvious too how entirely irrational this was.

Paralysis gripped the city. Some of the punishments ordered by the capital city, astonishingly, were interpreted as acts of revenge on behalf of the ladies themselves. The speaker who had so taken them to task was a case in point. "I would arrest the dog," said the Party chairman, "but those hags would be over the moon with delight. 'Look,' they would say, 'he insulted us, and see how he suffered!'"

There were more meetings on the subject. Meanwhile most people privately thought that this campaign should never have been started. Gentlemen were easy to deal with. You summoned them to court, found them guilty and chained them up. But you couldn't do anything to ladies. They rarely left their houses, only once, at most twice in as many months. They were as elusive as mirages.

When summer came to an end the Party chairman did not commit suicide as had been long expected but was dismissed, and this seemed an admission that the cause was lost.

But this conclusion was premature. The very moment of the ladies' apparent triumph proved the truth of the expression, "win a battle, but lose the war".

It was just after midday on 17 December when Madam Ganimet of the House of the Hankonats, dressed in her winter fur coat, tottered in her high heels across the inter-section of Varosh Street and the road to the *lycée*, when a woman greeted her from her right-hand side. "Good morning, Comrade Ganimet!"

The lady so addressed stopped in her tracks, as if struck by a blow. There for a moment she remained, in the middle of the crossroads and then slowly, as if trying to identify her assailant, attempted to turn her head. But her neck would not obey her.

"It's me, Comrade Ganimet. I'm Rosie, from the neighbourhood Committee. Are you coming along to the meeting tomorrow?"

Rosie's quarry remained rooted to the spot. Then she raised her hand as if in search of support and lifted it to her chest. Her knees trembled and she collapsed on the cobblestones.

Some passers-by contacted the hospital, which sent its only ambulance at once.

This was merely the start. Now that a hitherto unsuspected method of bringing down the indomitable ladies had been found, it was open season everywhere. Like seagulls at the end of their life span the ladies of the city fell one after another, wherever they were caught by the fatal cry of "Comrade!" The same scene was repeated: first they froze on the spot and reached out a despairing arm as if for support from some kind gentleman. Sir, your arm, please. Then there was an attempt to see where the blow had come from, a catch of the breath, a trembling at the knees, followed by collapse.

Mrs Nermin Fico and Mrs Sabeko of the House of Zekat both fell on the same day, the first as she was setting out from home and the second when returning from a social call. That same week it was the turn of Mrs Turtulli as she crossed Chain Square. A lady of the Kokalari House, emerging out of doors for the first time in two years, on hearing the cry of "Comrade!" tried to flee, but her knees gave way and she crumpled on the spot. Mrs Mukades Janina, rumoured at one time to have been the king's secret fiancée, slumped halfway across the Old Bridge, while her assailant, suddenly taking fright, ran away. A lady of the Çoçoli House managed to protest, "I'm not a comrade!" before she fainted, but others fell without a word. The two Maries, Marie Laboviti and Marie Kroi, could only manage an astonished cry of "Oaaah!", covering their mouths with their hands as they did when teased by street urchins; but this time they did not laugh.

And so it continued, on Castle Street, by the Powder Magazine, in front of Xuano's shop, by the State Bank and at Çerçiz Topulli Square, where in 1908 our hero Çerçiz shot the Turkish major, after challenging him, "Hey Turkish scum, here comes death from Çerçiz!" All over the town the ladies fell one by one.

Everyone noticed how few of them there were now.

Strangely, now that they were so much less visible, people thought about them more often, recalling places "where the incident happened", and other details, such as the case of Mrs Meriban Hashorva, carried home on an army stretcher, or Mrs Shtino, who after a gypsy girl shouted "Comrade!" expressed her dying wishes on the way to the hospital. At these "sites of incidents" a stonemason whose name was never mentioned was said to be putting up plaques with the names of the ladies and the day and exact time of their fall.

It was now universally understood that after all that had happened, the ladies had shut themselves up indoors, never to emerge again. Among them were Mrs Pekmezi and Mrs Karllashi, two ladies of the House of Shamet who used an old family alphabet for their correspondence, and also a lady of the Çabejs, another of the Fico family and finally an elderly Kadare lady with her sister, Nesibe Karagjozi.

Clearly the ladies were beaten.

DAY 2,000

The setting of their star brought no joy. Secretly, people felt remorse at this disruption of the natural order. There was a feeling that the ladies would be gone for a long time. It would take decades, if not centuries, for the great Houses to produce new ladies, for only these cultivated families possessed the expertise. Without them it was predicted that the city would turn savage, but nobody knew in what way. The code of the ladies' secrets had never been broken. Now their culture had been extinguished and it was impossible to say what might grow in the ashes they left behind.

Superficially the city remained the same. But to the much-abused surrounding villages and small towns, it seemed that the hour to settle scores had struck. Yet they did not dare. The city stood firm. With its ladies it had possibly held its head higher, but without them it seemed the more dangerous.

It now became clear that the city was unsuited not just to the new era but to any era. The news that it would be declared a "museum city" was welcomed as an honour by some, but the majority took it as a mark of shame. A third group tried to encourage hopes of the city's regeneration. Words beginning with 're-' appeared again, in feverish campaigns.

"Lunatics' Lane" was at the top of the list for renaming.

Some people thought this must mean demolishing the street, but this would not be easy. The principal obstacle was the house of the Leader of the new Albania, or rather its ruins, very close by. Families such as the Skëndulajs or the Shamets sometimes favoured and sometimes discouraged the demolition, while the Kadares' house, which was also nearby but at the opposite end of the street, only suggested sinister ideas. It was in fact the other Kadare house in the Hazmurat neighbourhood whose bad reputation had clung to it ever since its owner, to the family's shame, had gambled it away, but many people thought that it was this Kadare house in Palorto that would stain the city's name for ever and ever. Nobody knew the reasons for this prophecy, but precisely because they were unknown, the curse seemed the more credible. People said a fire or a heavy British bomber might be able to dispel its evil aura.

LATER. DAY 3,000

However far-fetched they might seem, all these rumours about "Lunatics' Lane", whether its renaming or its demolition or the demolition of the entire city, were no more than a pale reflection of the conspiracies, cabals and other horrors that were hatched that winter among the highest echelons of power. The Leader's drawn expression betrayed his fear of being overthrown but still he emerged the winner.

The decision to reconstruct his house to three times its original size was only one of the hopeful signs. The entire city's spirits lifted. It had deluded itself with its fears of reprisals and humiliation. The order of the day was now not to humiliate the city, but to praise it to the skies.

A piece of good news arrived to increase the general joy. Rumours were generally ominous but this was something genuinely different. The city expected some rare treat; of what kind, nobody knew, not even the municipal leaders. But still the news spread. Probably there would be a big celebration with an important guest from the highest possible level. The city was no backwater to be awed by a visit. Besides the Leader, whose birthplace it was, the city had received King Zog and the princesses, his sisters, as well as Benito Mussolini of Italy and Victor Emmanuel, who was not only King of Italy and Albania but also Emperor of Ethiopia.

There had also been non-visits that did not take place such as, at the beginning of the century, that of the Ottoman sultan with his mother, the valide sultan, whose marshal of the levée was also a native of the city. The most recent unrealised visit was that of Adolf Hitler, who was supposed to have come to inspect a plane that the city claimed to have invented, which worked on the principle of perpetual motion. But the outbreak of war had prevented this.

None of these visits or non-visits could compare with the one that was now expected. Stalin was coming.

This great news ushered in the new year of 1953. The cold was no less biting but the icicles hanging from the eaves of the houses glistened as if for Easter.

DAY 3,033

Everybody was caught up in the intoxication caused by this news. From morning to night the cafés speculated on the reason why Stalin had chosen Gjirokastër of all places. Most people thought that it did not take great minds to work this out: the city was the Leader's birthplace and it was well known that among all the leaders of the Communist Bloc outside of Russia, Stalin did not and could not have a more faithful devotee than the leader of Albania. Some suggested other reasons but only quietly and tentatively, mentioning for instance the ladies and how they had fallen. Among the thousands of cities in the Eastern Bloc, only ours had done away with its ladies.

For whatever reason, Gjirokastër would become for a few days the centre of the world. In fact, a secretly harboured desire of the city to become the centre of the planet just once was probably now coming out in the open.

As happens whenever people go too far, in the midst of the rejoicing it turned out that the city had been, as they say, riding for a fall. As January ended and February began, a dark thunderbolt struck: Stalin would not be coming.

After the first shock, when, having dreamed of being the summit of the world the city fell into a bottomless pit, a hail of questions fell. Why? Stalin must be angry, of course. This was the first guess, because anger caused most kinds of furore. He was no doubt angry at Gjirokastër, perhaps at Albania, if not the whole of Europe.

In 1908, when the sultan had cancelled his visit, it took several years to discover the reason, which turned out to be something that had not crossed anybody's mind: the alphabet. The sultan's court had protested that after the Ottoman Empire's centuries-old love affair with Albania, the latter had treacherously rejected the Arabic script in favour of the Latin alphabet!

Of course Stalin was greater and more daunting than the sultan, and his explosion of fury would also be greater and more devastating.

DAY 3,042

Nobody could remember a more bitterly cold February. In its first week, instead of brighter news or at least no news at all, a shock came when the two doctors, Big and Little Gurameto, were arrested once again. For the first time they were not weighed in the balance against each other. Both men were seized at midnight, clapped in steel handcuffs and taken to the same prison.

TIME TURNS BACK. DAY 3,029

Nobody knew who was the first to notice it, still less mention it. Time was not just suspended, as it had been for the anaesthetised hospital patients nine years before; it was going backwards at great speed.

All sorts of reasons were suggested. One was that Stalin was not ageing but growing younger, by some secret technique. Consequently time was flowing backwards, to match. Soon we would reach not 1954 but 1952, and so on: 1949, 1939, 1937. . .

There was no news of the doctors.

PART THREE

1953

CHAPTER NINE

Nobody had ever seen the Cave of Sanisha but everyone talked about it. The cave was universally imagined as the deepest and most terrifying dungeon of the city's prison, which was housed in the ancient castle that dominated Gjirokastër. It had been closed up since the time of Ali Pasha Tepelene, whose sister Sanisha gave it its name. This young woman had been kidnapped and raped and her assailants had been tortured in this cell for days and nights on end, while Ali Pasha himself watched through a secret spyhole.

Whenever governments turned nasty they used this cave as a threat, but people were sure that it would never be put to use again. So in that unforgettable February when there was talk of the Cave of Sanisha being opened, something else was in fact expected, perhaps the release of the two doctors. Everybody felt sure that they had been arrested in error. When the news came one evening that not only had their arrest been no mistake, but that after one hundred and fifty years of disuse the Cave of Sanisha would be their dungeon, the city was incredulous. The cave had not been opened after the murder of the Turkish prefect nor the suspected murder of the sultan's mother, the rebellion against the king nor even the conspiracy of the anti-communist members of parliament; but now it was to be used for the doctors.

The report turned out to be true. The cave had been specially equipped for them, and both the doctors were already inside it.

What condition were they in? Did they rest their heads on stones for pillows, did anyone think to cover them with blankets? Both Gurametos, wasting in prison! Were they chained to the wall like the rapists of long ago? Was salt rubbed into the wounds of their tortured bodies? Or were they well treated with champagne and music?

All sorts of strange questions were asked before anybody thought of the most important one: what had they done?

At first it was hard to find anything to accuse them of but soon it became easy enough. Just as the world was swept with wind and rain, so it was burdened with guilt. A share could be allotted to the doctors with plenty left over for others.

Meanwhile these frantic attempts to conjure up a crime were interrupted by the arrival of two investigators. Shaqo Mezini and Arian Ciu were two young men from the city, fresh graduates of the Dzerzhinsky Academy of the secret police in Moscow. Their faces were pale, their ties tightly knotted and their overcoats extremely long. The godfather of the secret police who gave his name to the academy had proverbially worn a coat like this and had said, "Long coat, short shrift."

The two investigators became the visible dimension of the Gurameto case. The doctors were below in the dark of the pit but at least the investigators bobbed above the surface like balloons, signals from the lower depths.

On Tuesday, 13 February, the two investigators emerged from the Cave of Sanisha clutching their files and strode purposefully down Hamurati Street, heading not for the police station but the hospital.

Remzi Kadare was at the gate, his expression menacing and his face distorted with senseless fury. He wagged his finger. "Whatever happens here isn't my fault. If you want to find the guilty ones, look at the other Kadares from Palorto." He lowered his voice. "Oh no, what's going on? They're up to no good."

The investigators listened in puzzlement and then crossed the hospital yard, watched by the doctors and nurses standing at the entrance.

The examination of the two doctors' operation records, or rather, the full list of their patients, caused no concern. On the contrary, a wave of relief swept through the entire hospital. This first ray of light shed on the mystery roused some hope. They were looking at the mortality rate of operations. Everywhere in the world people died during surgery, their families complained about the doctors, the doctors justified themselves and the cases went to court.

The investigators spent more than four hours in the hospital registry. Before they had passed the main gate, where Remzi Kadare again stood ready to say something that to him was very important, the first results of the investigation became known. Of the twelve thousand and more operations carried out by Big Dr Gurameto, about one thousand eight hundred patients had died on the operating table or soon after. The number for Little Dr Gurameto was less than one thousand. (The tendency to compare the two was again apparent.)

The investigation of the two doctors, like many things where they were concerned, took place on two levels. The first, in the Cave of Sanisha, was hidden from everybody. The second and visible dimension involved the hospital, the morgue, family homes and sometimes the cemetery. Records of autopsies and personal interviews were attached to the medical records.

The investigators, now pale after sleepless nights, appeared less often in the city. They lost weight, making their overcoats seem even longer. What was called the public side of the investigation now had its own secret aspects, which strangely did not relate to the dead but to the living. One by one, surviving patients, or rather their surgical scars, were to be examined for the oddest things, such as stitches in the form of six-pointed stars, tattoos, and old symbols (Hebrew ones for instance) of mysterious import.

Some called these stories crazy but others replied, "Wait, just wait and you'll see. This business will go far. This is serious stuff." Since the two doctors were not only surgeons but gynaecologists, women would also be subjected to intimate examinations.

Listeners to foreign radio stations, especially the BBC, passed on an extraordinary piece of news: a group of terrorist doctors had been exposed in the Kremlin, the very citadel of communism. The Soviets themselves had broadcast the news, calling it "murder in a white coat". The usual furore was absent, probably because the case spoke for itself, but the report shocked the entire planet. Under the direction of a Jewish organisation known as the "Joint", a group of doctors was preparing the greatest crime in the history of mankind: the elimination by murder of all the communist leaders throughout the world, starting with Joseph Stalin.

This incomparable crime would change world history. The globe would tilt on its axis and not regain its balance for a thousand years, if ever. So Stalin's anger, which had been thought to be directed at Gjirokastër, was in fact aimed at the whole world.

A small, hesitant voice ventured to say that perhaps he was angry at both Gjirokastër *and* the world.

At first it seemed a nonsensical idea to link the plot to Gjirokastër but now it was the natural and obvious thing. The conspiracy, although first discovered in the Kremlin, had stretched its tentacles everywhere: Hungary, East Germany, Poland, Albania, even Mongolia.

People's brains worked feverishly. So there was some truth in the stories about Stalin's rejuvenation, time in reverse gear, the years moving backwards and that semi-official notice of a visit by the Father of the Peoples.

There were two interpretations of this visit. According to the first, Stalin really had intended to come. The headquarters of the "Joint", having long ago made its preparations to strike on Stalin's first visit abroad, had issued orders to its cell in Albania, that is in Gjirokastër, to stand ready. The conspirators would poke out their heads like moles, and would suffer the consequences.

In the second version the announcement of a visit was a front. It would never take place, and the "Joint" headquarters and Gjirokastër itself would fall into a trap. But still the moles would poke out their heads, and suffer. In either case Gjirokastër would pay a heavy cost for its vainglory. The city's name was whispered everywhere. The entire communist world seethed with orders, warnings, secret communiqués.

At three in the afternoon on 16 February, Blind Vehip was clapped in handcuffs at the crossroads of Varosh Street, in full view of the astonished passers-by.

With her face as white as plaster, in a long dress on which there was no trace of violence, she approached the village. She walked slowly, yet not with downcast head as expected but with a distant expression, everything about her suggesting detachment.

That is how they had seen her leaving the village of Kardhiq, where for three days and nights they had stripped her of her humanity, and that is how she looked as they watched her coming to Tepelene. Those who had heard her story from others, who themselves had it from hearsay, had imagined her looking like this, or even paler. A song had been composed about her, though nobody knew when or by whom. It began, "I lost my soul in the prison cell/Of Sanisha, black as hell."

As she walked, her brother Ali Tepelene watched her from his great house through a long officer's telescope. His face was as black with fury as hers was pale. His sister's movements made it clear that she had come to look for death. No doubt at his hands. He did what she wanted and coldly shot her, first with a bullet in the forehead, and then with two, one in the forehead and one in the heart, and then four, fourteen, God knows how many. But this brought him no peace of mind. He killed her again, with all kinds of weapons, but still he was not satisfied, only filled with such distress that when he saw her dead, he kissed her on the brow.

Later when he heard the song, he said to himself, "Ah, why didn't I kill her properly?"

No one know who had composed the song, and its meaning was ambiguous: it could be interpreted as a song of her ravishers, shackled in the Cave of Sanisha, in the cell which her avenging brother had later created especially for them; it might equally be taken as a song about the fatal depths of a woman's body, below her belly, which had led them into temptation. But in both cases it was a song or lament put into the mouths of her violators. Ali Tepelene, the most powerful vezir of the Ottoman Empire, who would give orders even to the sultan, had been unable in forty years to detach the meaning of the song from its dark history.

On 17 February, shortly before midnight, Shaqo Mezini and Arian Ciu, the foremost investigators of Albania and perhaps of the entire Communist Bloc, could not rid their minds of this song; its words made their knees buckle with terror and desire as they descended the steps of the famous cave.

They led the two doctors, whom they had known since childhood, in handcuffs.

A blinding light shone from an electric torch.

Neither of the investigators knew what their voices would sound like under the stone vault. When they first spoke, the sound was even stranger than they expected.

They heard their words, not in their own voices but as if spoken by actors from the distant past, returning to them enveloped in a terrifying echo and hanging suspended in the chamber before they melted away. "For ... the ... m u r d e r ..."

It took some time for the doctors to understand the language. They were under investigation for the murder of patients during surgical procedures. They had no way of questioning why. There were no whys and hows. They were supposed to listen carefully to the conclusion of the investigation. This was a democratic proletarian state with the highest form of justice in the world, which never punished the innocent. The doctors were now cleared of the accusation of murder. The investigators had examined the full list of their patients and the exact times of their murders, they meant their deaths, and in particular the biographies of the victims, or rather the deceased, and had concluded that the numbers of the deceased of different political allegiances, i.e. communists, royalists and nationalists, did not reveal any political bias on the part of the surgeons. The suspicions against them were totally groundless.

The doctors sighed in relief but the investigators did not look any more relaxed. "We have only one question. It is simple, but fundamental."

After a long silence the question was finally put to the two prisoners. The investigators now knew that the doctors had not committed murder. But the question was, were they aware ...

Almost in unison the doctors exclaimed, "*What?*" And indeed the astonished Big Dr Gurameto said it in German, "*Was?*"

The investigators tried to explain. The word "aware" need not be interpreted in a literal sense. They meant a general awareness that medicine could be used to commit murder. Political murder, of course. For instance of communist leaders.

The same gasps of amazement came again, and an exclamation in German.

Never. Of course not. They were doctors. They were bound by the Hippocratic oath. Who would dare suggest something so repellent, even as a joke?

"Our interview is over," said one of the investigators. "As you see, we have been impartial. We only wanted the truth. Guard, take the prisoners to their cells."

Two hours later, at three in the morning, they brought the doctors back to the cave. Not only the investigators' voices but everything else was different. The cave had become their home. In fact the investigators' first words were, "I think you know that we are here in the Cave of Sanisha."

The doctors nodded to show they did.

Both sides stared at each other. "Don't think we're taking back what we said two hours ago, that we hoodwinked you and just pretended to believe in your innocence. There's no question of that. You're clear of any charge of murder. We're going to ask you about something else."

The investigators felt that the cave had taken them into its power. A fervour and excitement that they had never felt before, in which lust and suffering were mixed, had totally mastered them. They were not just investigators, they were the ravishers of Ali Pasha Tepelene's sister. They were both torturers and their own victims.

"Dr Gurameto, we want to ask you about the dinner on the night of 16 September 1943."

More than anything that had been said so far, this sent a chill of terror through the doctor.

Ah, that dinner. He did not say these words aloud, but they were in his eyes, his laboured breath, the very hair on his head.

The investigators looked straight at him.

"What do you want to know?" Dr Gurameto said, but in a voice that seemed to question whether what had happened could ever be known.

"We want the truth," the investigators said, almost in one voice. "Everything. Hour by hour and minute by minute."

The doctor stared into vacant space.

Could this truth ever be known or put in words? So far every effort had been made to conceal it. For almost ten years, by unspoken agreement, these events had been covered by the cold ash of oblivion, forgotten by both Germans and Albanians, royalists, nationalists and communists alike. Now they wanted to wipe away this ash. They wanted the truth.

"The whole truth," the investigators repeated. "What happened. What was said. What was not said."

Big Dr Gurameto lowered his eyelids. The doctor began to speak, slowly and tonelessly. The square in front of the city hall with its wet asphalt and the statue of Çerçiz Topulli in the middle appeared before him with extraordinary distinctness. The tank crews had just descended to stretch their legs. The officers fussed over the mud that spattered their boots. Then, by the door of an armoured vehicle, he saw Colonel Fritz von Schwabe, the commander of the troops, with his army greatcoat slung over his shoulder. His college friend watched him with glistening eyes as he approached.

Their emotional greeting. What von Schwabe said: 'Do you recognise me? Have I changed?' Then his dismay at Albanian treachery, his threat to punish the city, the hostages. As threatening as anything he said was the pale glint of his Iron Cross.

Dr Gurameto asked if it was necessary to relate in detail what happened next. The investigators replied that he should tell what he thought was necessary, so he described his invitation, the colonel's acceptance and the dinner itself. He gave an account of who was present and of the atmosphere, the music and the champagne; he did not dwell any more than necessary on the release of the hostages. After he finished describing daybreak and how everybody was exhausted after the long night without sleep, there fell a long silence that was finally broken by Shaqo Mezini with a single ominous question.

"Is that all?"

Dr Gurameto said nothing. The other investigator bent down by his shoulder and murmured softly in an almost caressing voice, "What you have told us is accurate. But we know these things. We want the rest of the story. What we don't know. The mystery."

Gurameto froze. The investigators watched him, but their expectations were dashed. With a jerk of his head, as if to banish all inner uncertainty of his own, he said, "There's no mystery."

Shaqo Mezini straightened his back against the metal chair. "Doctor, I'm sorry to have to say this, but you're not telling the truth."

Gurameto gave the investigator a cold look.

"I know something different," the investigator said, shaking his head as if to convey that saying this gave him a kind of pleasure that went beyond an investigator's professional satisfaction.

Big Dr Gurameto's eyes conceded defeat.

An intoxicating thrill swept through Shaqo Mezini. He had not realised how eagerly he had been waiting for this moment. At times of weakness, when he lost faith in the investigation's prospects of success, he was more scared that the doctor would not give in than of his superiors' displeasure. From the first day when he had learned that the doctor was part of this case, all his thoughts, obscurely, inexplicably, had focused obsessively on the figure of the prisoner. He had seen him dozens of times on Varosh Street, setting off for the hospital, an aloof, imposing figure. The investigator's secret dream was to become a person like this, held in regard by everybody but not regarding anybody himself. He knew that he was not the only person to revere the doctor like this and was aware that his aura came from his reputation as a surgeon, from having studied in Germany, and the many stories told about him.

Later, when he returned from the academy in Moscow to find this provincial city shorn of all its glamour, he was startled to discover that Big Dr Gurameto's aura, and that of his little counterpart, had survived undiminished. The young investigator was now conscious of this attraction, and that it was mixed with an element of anxiety. The big doctor was still unapproachable but now also seemed opposed to him. Shaqo Mezini found it hard to grasp the idea that he felt men like Big Dr Gurameto were in fact a block to him. It wasn't even that they stood in the way of new ideas, the construction of socialism and the like; their opposition, though Shaqo Mezini could not know it, resulted from something deeper. It was intrinsic to men of Shaqo Mezini's kind, something infinitely ruthless, like every kind of male rivalry.

Dr Gurameto was in Shaqo Mezini's way. With his scalpels in his hand and wearing his white mask, he had acquired a stature that nobody could diminish. Moreover, he was a gynaecologist. To Shaqo Mezini's mind, this meant having power over women, especially beautiful women, who submitted to him. A master of women! This was precisely what Shaqo Mezini was not. He was not ugly but neither was he sufficiently handsome to attract beautiful women. He had had a few ordinary exploits but never with women of real beauty, and there was never a question of having them in his power. But Gurameto ruled them, without possessing them. They came to him of their own accord, the investigator was sure, and he had no need to visit them. Perhaps his hand had even gone below the belly of Shaqo's own mother.

All these thoughts rolled through his mind like lowering storm clouds, and on the day when he was summoned and told that Big Dr Gurameto would be under his investigation, these clouds suddenly burst. He had never felt so excited. His elation was mixed with a kind of savagery. The stark thought now came to his mind that Big Gurameto had been a general impediment, an impediment to Shaqo Mezini in particular, and that he still stood in his way. In every sense.

Shaqo Mezini's thirst for revenge was inseparably

bound to a feeling of fear. Of course he had the doctor before him in handcuffs but still he did not feel safe. For some reason he felt that these handcuffs might make the doctor all the more dangerous. Shaqo Mezini could not persuade himself that Big Dr Gurameto too might feel frightened. He cast sidelong glances at the instruments of torture, kept in an alcove since the time of Sanisha, but not even these offered reassurance. This doctor had terrified thousands of patients with his surgical tools. How could he feel fear?

The investigator was convinced not only that Dr Gurameto was fearless but that he could not lie. Fear and lying were connected. When Shaqo Mezini came face to face with the surgeon for the first time, a sudden onset of terror drove out any emotion of anger against his enemy. The surgeon was shackled and his face was drawn and despairing, but still he showed no fear.

Shaqo Mezini was ashamed to realise that deep down he wanted to rouse not his enemy's hostility but his sympathy, and this he tried to convey to him in an almost subliminal message. "I'm sorry for you, but I can't do anything about it. Talk, put an end to your suffering. Save us all."

And then, as if responding to this covert appeal, the miracle-working surgeon, a legend in the city, caved in. At the critical moment he committed an act of suicide: he uttered a lie. Throughout that endless day the two investigators and their superiors had liaised with *their* superiors in Tirana, and these superiors had liaised with the other leaders of the great Communist Bloc, perhaps with Stalin himself. An aircraft had already reached Tirana and was expected to continue its flight to the airport of Gjirokastër. Now there was no room for doubt; the first crack had finally appeared in the doctor's story.

The investigators could hardly contain their joy.

Shaqo Mezini's first impulse was to leap to his feet, fill his lungs with air and shout in triumph. At last everything had fallen into place. Dr Gurameto had given in and Shaqo Mezini, not only a young investigator but also a young male, had gained the upper hand.

How grateful he felt to the Communist party that had worked this miracle.

His glance slid again to the antiquated instruments of torture that were now to be used on the manacled prisoner.

"Dr Gurameto," he announced in a firm voice of command. "Big Dr Gurameto, as they call you, isn't what you have just told us rather hard to believe? You have described an emotional reunion with an old college friend after many years. This close friend, by an amazing coincidence, turned out to be the commander of the German troops invading Albania. Isn't it a bit like of one of those old fairy tales we learned at school? Quite apart from the dinner with music and champagne, the release of the hostages and the salvation of the city, doesn't it look a bit like a game? Why not stop this charade and tell us what was really behind it?"

"I'm not playing a game," Gurameto said, looking him straight in the eye. "This isn't a charade. I don't behave like that."

The investigators now stared at him in outright mockery. Shaqo Mezini's only anxiety was that Dr Gurameto, having fallen into this morass, might find a way to climb out of it. But fortunately he was only sinking deeper.

"And if it turns out that it was a game? If we prove it?"

Gurameto shook his head again, this time in contempt.

The investigators were clearly waiting for something. They looked at their wristwatches and whispered to each other, but none of this made any impression on Gurameto. They repeated in flat, weary voices more or less what they had already asked. Had there been an ulterior purpose, or not, to the dinner on the night of 16 September? The investigators were now obviously impatient, and mentioned an aircraft. The plane from Tirana was delayed but it would certainly arrive, if only just before dawn.

During the course of the interrogation the investigators remembered that Little Dr Gurameto was also there. All this time he had been handcuffed by the left wrist to the other doctor's right hand but he had not uttered a word for hours. Two or three times the investigators had been about to ask him something, but thinking that he had not been present at the events of that day, or perhaps simply because they were tired, they forgot about him.

Both sides were succumbing to exhaustion. They heard muffled sounds from the entrance to the cave. Then came footsteps and the tapping of a cane, like a blind man's. The investigators were so tired that they entirely forgot Little Doctor Gurameto, who seemed to have evaporated like a ghost in front of their eyes. The two doctors had merged into one.

Big Dr Gurameto was experiencing something similar, except that the two investigators were not turning into one but had become three. "So there are three investigators," he thought. "But thirteen won't drag a word out of me."

The three figures hovered before him as if in a mist and one of them stammered some words in German.

Upon hearing a sudden noise the doctor opened his eyes for a moment, and he realised that this was not a dream. There really were three investigators in front of him, and one was speaking German. For the second time he was addressed with the words, "mein Herr".

Gurameto shivered. An ashen light filtered through a crevice in the cave. Perhaps it was dawn. They were all fully awake now.

"Grosse Herr Gurameto," said the newly-arrived investigator. "I am an officer of the Staatssicherheit, the security service of the East German Republic."

The man's German reached the doctor's ears even more indistinctly than the investigators' Albanian. The German said that he had flown from Berlin to interrogate him. He said that in the entire communist camp, there was no more important case than this. He invited the doctor to consider it seriously.

"I know of no other way," Gurameto replied.

The German investigator had been briefed about the case and asked the doctor to tell him in a very few words what had happened on the day of 16 September 1943 and the following night.

Dr Gurameto nodded. He replied in German, the language of the question, and his account was as detailed as before.

When he had finished, the third investigator asked quietly, "Is that the truth?"

"Yes," the prisoner replied.

The silence was insupportable. Then Gurameto noticed

another figure, an interpreter whispering into the ears of the two Albanian investigators.

"What you have just said is not the truth," said the German.

Dr Gurameto's expression did not change.

"The German officer, Colonel Fritz von Schwabe, whom you insist that you met on 16 September 1943, was not in Albania at the time you claim."

The German's voice sank lower. Not taking his eyes off the handcuffed prisoner, he said that Fritz von Schwabe had not been present on Albanian soil or indeed any other kind, because he had been buried four months before.

Gurameto's face turned wan.

The other man explained that Colonel Fritz von Schwabe had died of wounds in a field hospital in the Ukraine on 11 May 1943. The investigator had brought his death certificate and photographs that showed the colonel in the hospital, and his funeral.

"There's no need to go on," Gurameto interrupted in a broken voice. His head suddenly fell forward, as if struck by a blow at the back of the neck. "I need to sleep," he added after a moment. "Please."

The investigators exchanged glances.

CHAPTER TEN

The uproar caused by what was called the conspiracy of the century spread across the entire planet. The investigation was conducted by eleven communist states, in twenty-seven languages and thirty-nine dialects, not to mention subdialects. About four hundred doctors imprisoned in as many cells were subjected to continuous interrogation.

None of the inmates of these cells received any news from outside, and those outside were ignorant of the cells. The Cave of Sanisha was only one cell among many.

At noon the following day the three investigators, with the interpreter a shadowy presence behind them, paid another visit to the two handcuffed prisoners in the cave.

"The truth was . . . the truth is that I suspected from the very start that it wasn't him."

Gurameto's first words crept slowly out of his mouth and were swallowed up by the echoing vault. He squinted in an effort to recall the time more clearly, casting his mind back to the square of the city hall, the wet asphalt and the tank crew who went up to the window of the closed café and raised their hands to their brows like peaked caps as they tried to see inside.

An aide had nodded towards one of the armoured

vehicles, where the officer was waiting. On the way to the square the aide had told Gurameto explicitly, "The regimental commander, your friend from university, is waiting for you by the city hall."

The colonel stood leaning against the armoured vehicle, in dark glasses, with one leg crossed over the other. Gurameto, even before he was close to him, felt his chest tighten with a spasm of doubt. After his greeting, "Don't you recognise me?" the same spasm came again. His voice had changed. The man smiled and pointed to his face; it did not need a surgeon to notice the scars.

"Four wounds," said the colonel, as the two spread their arms to embrace one another.

Of course the scars made a difference, Gurameto thought. But there were other things too. The uniform, the passage of fifteen years, the war.

The doctor described their conversation to his interrogators almost exactly as before: the colonel's disappointment at the treachery of the Albanians and their violation of the laws of hospitality enshrined in the *Kanun of Lekë Dukagjini*, the threat of taking hostages and finally his own invitation to dinner.

He described the dinner in the same way, now dwelling on certain details, like the donning of the masks. This had been a fashion of the time at student dinners when the men were at university, even if he could not remember Fritz von Schwabe following it. Nor could he understand why the other man put on a mask and then took it off. Of course, from time to time the doctor's suspicions had been aroused, especially when he caught out his guest in some error of fact. But he had put these doubts out of his mind for the reasons he had explained: the passage of time, his career in the army, the war. The doctor also said more about the following morning. His daughter, seeing them all asleep where they had fallen, thought that her father had poisoned his guests alongside his own family. He himself suspected his daughter of the same thing.

But now for the first time he mentioned his later suspicions. He never saw the German again. He tried once to meet him but was told that he was busy. On another occasion when he enquired after him he was told that there was nobody by the name of Fritz von Schwabe. He discovered later and only by chance that von Schwabe had been transferred elsewhere on duty. After that he heard nothing more.

The prisoner hung his head as a sign that his story was over. But a moment later he added that the other side had probably also deplored the dinner.

"What?" said the investigators almost together.

"I said that the Germans too may have disapproved of the dinner."

"Aha."

The silence was so protracted that everybody was sure that there was no more to say. The investigators whispered for a while among themselves. Shaqo Mezini was the first to speak.

"My question is a simple one: Why? A man arrives from far away, commanding the first regiment to enter another country and suddenly takes it into his head to change his name and pretend to be someone else. What is he up to?"

The handcuffed prisoner shrugged his shoulders. He had no idea.

The investigator's voice rose, resonating through the cave. "What was he thinking of? How could he find the time, in such conditions, exposed to so many dangers, to invent this tale of a college friend and come for dinner? Was it his prank, or yours? Or were you both involved? Tell me."

"I don't know," replied the prisoner. "Perhaps it was his game. But not mine."

"Gurameto. Don't try to wriggle out of this. It wasn't a game, but something much deeper. Tell us!"

"I don't know."

"You knew you would meet him. You had agreed between yourselves. You had codes, masks, false names. Talk!"

"No."

"Do you recognise this writing? This name?"

The German investigator had interrupted, producing a short letter in German that ended with the words "Jerusalem, February 1949" and was signed "Dr Jakoel".

"I know this man," the prisoner replied. "He was my colleague. He was a pharmacist in the city, a Jew. He left for Palestine in 1946."

"What else?"

"He was one of the hostages released that night."

"Aha, a Nazi colonel, a bearer of the Iron Cross, releases the first Jew he captures in Albania. Why? Sprich!"

The prisoner shrugged his shoulders.

"Herr Gurameto, I haven't flown two thousand kilometres to listen to ravings in a medieval cave. Let me repeat the question. Why?"

"Because I asked him to."

"Aha. And why did you ask him? And why did he listen to you? Sprich!"

"Because we were, according to him, college friends."

"College friends or something else? Sprich!"

"I don't know what to say."

"Herr Gurameto, do you know what the 'Joint' is?"

"No. I've never heard of it."

"Let me tell you," Shaqo Mezini interrupted. "It's a long-standing Jewish organisation. A murderous sect, whose aim is to establish Jewish rule throughout the world."

"I've never heard of it."

"Their next crime, their most horrible crime, was to be the murder of the leaders of world communism, starting with Stalin."

"I've never . . . "

"That's enough. Don't interrupt. And now talk!"

"Sprich!"

"Never . . . "

"That's enough."

"You're not letting me speak."

"Speak!"

The investigators started a crossfire of questions.

"There is a mystery, I admit," said Gurameto. "But you can work it out yourselves. You have the means. You have the real name of this person who pretended to be a dead man. Perhaps you have the man himself."

"That's enough! You're here to answer questions, not ask them. Speak!"

"I don't know what to say."

"Then we'll force you. We have the means to do that."

The eyes of first the investigators and then the prisoner wandered to the corner with the antique instruments of torture: hooks, knives, pincers to gouge out eyes, pliers to grip testicles. Witnesses had testified that it was the tortures effected by the pliers that Ali Pasha Tepelene particularly liked to watch through a spyhole in the wall.

The investigators whispered again among themselves.

"Dr Gurameto," said Shaqo Mezini, no longer hiding the fact that he was in charge. "Despite our differences, we hope we will come to an understanding. As you can see, our suspicions relate to a terrible and macabre crime. The State requires us to be suspicious. For its own protection, of course. We don't believe that you are its enemy; you have worked for it for years. You don't want to see this State overthrown any more than we do. Is that true? Speak!"

The prisoner shrugged his shoulders again.

"The matter is simple. We want to know what lies behind this story. What was this game from the very start? What really happened at that dinner? Where did the orders come from? What were your secret signals and codes? I hardly need remind you that we're dealing with a worldwide conspiracy in which you played a part, perhaps unwittingly. Speak!"

The prisoner raised his head. He moved his lips several times as if testing them before he spoke. "You think the German colonel was part of this conspiracy? And me too?

"Why not?

"I had no part in it. I know nothing about it. There's your answer."

"Did it cross your mind, even for a moment, that your dinner guest was . . . a dead man?"

This question came from the other investigator, who had been silent so far that night.

The prisoner screwed up his eyes. "As I said, I suspected

it wasn't him. And also, but only for a moment, that he was dead. It was a well-known story in the city, passed down by our grandmothers. You couldn't help thinking of it."

"Aha, go on."

"I can prove that I suspected it. I have a living witness."

"We know," the investigator interrupted. "Blind Vehip. We know everything."

"I thought that as soon as you arrested him."

"Go on! Keep talking!"

Gurameto went on to describe his conversation with the blind man under the pale street lamp at the intersection of Varosh Street and the road to the *lycée*. As he talked he couldn't help thinking of the interrogation they must have carried out, their questions and the blind man's answers. "You're not telling the truth, old man. Where did you get the idea that Dr Gurameto had invited a dead man to dinner? Speak!" "I don't know what to say. It just came into my head." "You're blind. You've never seen either the living or the dead. How can you tell the difference when you have no eyes?" "I don't know. Perhaps just because . . ." "What? Speak!" "Perhaps it's just because I'm blind."

His own questioning of the blind man nine years ago was where this interrogation had started. Now it was being turned against him. The investigators were repeating it word for word.

The prisoner raised his hand to his brow. In a quiet voice he said that he needed to pull himself together.

Of course he had suspected all the time that his guest was not what he claimed to be, and during the dinner especially. There had been moments when the two men had been on the point of admitting it to each other. "My dear unforgotten friend, aren't you in fact dead?" And the other man's reply. "Yes, but how could you tell? Of course I am."

Again the prisoner said he was not trying to hide anything. The secret that eluded him lay in the events themselves.

Strangely, the investigators did not interrupt him.

Ever since he had seen the colonel leaning against the armoured vehicle on the square of the city hall, two contrary thoughts had been at war inside him. Was it him or not? This man resembled his old college friend, but at the same time did not. The doctor thought of the moment when the disciples saw the risen Christ. His body was that of Jesus and yet was not. That was how the scriptures described it, *soma pneumatikon*, a spiritual or ethereal body.

Gurameto saw in the investigators' faces that the mention of Christ caused not just irritation but fear. Perhaps this was why they hadn't interrupted him.

Everything was like that, as if on two planes, the prisoner went on to explain. Sometimes he took the colonel to be a dead man, and indeed at times the colonel had seemed on the point of revealing himself as such. That donning and removal of the mask had probably even been a sign to him, which he had failed to understand.

"A sign," Shaqo Mezini muttered.

The investigators looked at each other. For the first time, the prisoner had admitted that the conspirator had given him a sign.

It was now past three o'clock in the morning. Gurameto, his voice faint from exhaustion, was saying that the dead man had probably come to him in a shape that was in accordance with the laws of his world and brought signs from it. That was why there was so much mystery and misunderstanding.

The prisoner said he was no longer in a fit state. He would try to say more tomorrow.

After a whispered consultation, the investigators told him he could rest.

After the plane that had brought the German investigator, for the second time that week a light aircraft landed at the city's airport. The airport had been virtually abandoned for ten years and this increase in traffic was striking. The first time, they barely managed to clear the runway of weeds and there had been no question of landing lights. In anticipation of the aircraft's arrival, men holding torches had stood for hours in the February cold. Fortunately this second plane landed in the afternoon. At the last moment the wind from the Tepelene Gorge to the north of the city, as keen as ever, almost brought it down.

Clearly something extraordinary was happening, but few associated it with the interrogation in the Cave of Sanisha.

The man who disembarked from the second aircraft was a Russian investigator. His German counterpart with his gaunt, lined face had been a formidable presence, but this Russian looked unassuming. He was portly, almost bald and walked with an avuncular amble.

Shaqo Mezini and Arian Ciu came to the airport to meet him. At first they were visibly disappointed, but their conversation with him as they walked from the runway to the little airport building made them change their minds. They quickly realised that this person must be important. They all spoke fluently in Russian and before even reaching the hotel, the two Albanian investigators felt certain that this man had come straight from the Kremlin.

They talked in a secluded corner of the hotel. The Russian grasped the situation at once, as if he had been dealing with the case for years. He had come to provide assistance. He made it clear that he had experience of trials in Moscow that had been kept from the public.

The Albanians described for him how the investigation stood. They told him about the German investigator's help, about the moments when they hoped the doctors would crack and other aspects of the case about which they did not feel so confident.

The Russian gave extraordinarily detailed instructions. In the first session they would test the prisoners' sincerity, especially Big Dr Gurameto's. Everything else depended on this. They would try to obtain precise answers to certain questions. What had the doctor and his foreign guest said in their private conversations during the dinner? What did the doctor know about German intentions towards Albania? There had been talk of secret discussions before the invasion with a group of pro-German Albanians who would take over the country's government. What had been Dr Gurameto's role in this group, if any? Why had he felt in such a strong position, almost equal to the German colonel? Where had he found the courage to speak up for the hostages, especially Jakoel the Jew? What did the Germans think about their massacre of civilians at the village of Borova? Did they feel remorse? Or did they pretend to?

Who had waved that white sheet as a sign of the city's surrender? If there was no truth in this story of the white sheet, who made it up, the Albanians or the Germans?

The two Albanians were reluctant to interrupt the Russian, but expressed their surprise. So far they had thought they were investigating the great Jewish plot, but now they were being asked about the German occupation.

As their discussion came to an end, the Russian investigator's eyes gleamed. He understood what the Albanians were trying to say, but he was leading up to this. Testing the prisoner's sincerity was merely a preparation for the final stage. First they had to make it clear to him that there was nothing that they didn't know.

The Russian explained that the revelation of private conversations was the most effective of all possible methods of interrogation. The prisoner might imagine all kinds of things, but never that they could know what he said in private. When he realised that they did, he would be overcome with terror.

The Albanian investigators stared at the Russian in admiration.

"Don't look so astonished," the Russian said. "I know my job and this is no bluff. We know all these things, maybe better than the prisoner does himself. For instance, we might remind him of the phrase he used, 'I'm not Albania, Fritz, just as you aren't Germany. We're something else.'"

"Excuse me," said Shaqo Mezini. "This means that Fritz von Schwabe is still alive and he has told you of the events of that night."

"No," the Russian butted in. "He's dead. Our German colleagues have confirmed this."

The Russian's clear eyes glittered with enthusiasm. The mysterious colonel really had died, but for the moment the two Albanians need not be told anything more. He knew from experience that premature revelations spoilt the proceedings. For the moment they should concentrate on this matter of private conversations. They were the key to everything.

The next interrogation session would be decisive. The prisoner had promised to talk. The Russian investigator would watch through that same hole in the wall that Ali Pasha Tepelene had used, following for entire nights the torture of the men who had raped his sister.

"Good God, he even knows about that," muttered Arian Ciu.

"What?" asked the Russian. The Albanians' awe of him was obvious, and again their visitor's glassy eyes glistened.

CHAPTER ELEVEN

At midnight Big Dr Gurameto was led into the Cave of Sanisha alone. This was the first time he had been interrogated without the little doctor. The handcuffs which had tied him to the other man's right hand dangled from his wrist and his movements were clumsy. Without his colleague he felt an empty space beside him.

"You promised to talk," Shaqo Mezini said softly.

The prisoner nodded.

The questioning that night was long and tiring but the investigators did not intervene as they had in other sessions, when they had thought that a crossfire of interruptions was the best way to unsettle their victim. They now realised that not interrupting was just as disorienting.

It struck the doctor that they were making him talk with the express purpose of wearing him down. He told them what he knew about the secret talks with the Germans before the invasion. Of course the Germans had kept a file on Albania and had their people in place. The group of German sympathisers was large. The cream of the nationalist elite, as they were known, all either had a German cultural background or supported the Germans. They included Mehdi and Mit'hat Frashëri, from the most famous Albanian family of all; the great Albanian linguist Eqrem Çabej; the country's most admired poet, Lasgush Poradeci; Father Anton Harapi, a figure of uncompromised moral stature; the renowned scholar, Lef Nosi; the distinguished Kosovo politician Rexhep Mitrovica and dozens of others.

Gurameto, the celebrated surgeon, expected them to ask him where he stood, so he told them himself. He had known many of these people but he did not count himself among this elite and still less was he a collaborator, any more than Çabej and Poradeci were. He did not hide that he had been inclined, tempted, like many who had studied in Germany, but this should not be confused with Nazism. It was an attraction to Germany, as was only natural. A lot of things were not as clear then as they later became. He was a surgeon and sometimes he performed ten operations in one day. He had no time for anything else. He would come home at midnight still wearing his white coat.

Finally they butted in to remind him that the question was about the secret talks before the invasion.

Of course he had heard about them, and in fact knew a good deal. The Germans had made preparations, knowing they would enter Albania sooner or later. So they had discussed certain matters in advance with their sympathisers in Albania. The essential point was that the Germans would come as liberators and not an occupying power. This meant observing certain conditions: there would be no murderous reprisals and the customs of the country would be respected, especially where Albanian honour and women were concerned. The doctor was aware of these things.

One of the investigators broke in to ask if this

knowledge had given him the courage to demand the release of the hostages.

Of course, the prisoner replied. He was almost certain that the Germans would ask for the massacre of Borova to be forgotten and promise that such a thing would not happen again.

But what about the release of Jakoel the Jew? How had he been so bold as to ask for this? It was well known that nobody at that time dared ask for the release of a Jew.

The eyes of the investigators and the prisoner met for a moment.

It was a matter of respect for local customs. To the doctor's knowledge, the Jewish question had been one of the most delicate aspects of the talks. The politicians who were to take over the government of Albania had dug in their heels over the Jews.

"So now you're singing the praises of the Quislings!" the investigators pounced, speaking together.

"I'm not praising anybody. I know that the communists too insisted that the Jews would not be harmed."

"We shot these Quislings afterwards," Shaqo Mezini said. "You know that perfectly well: Father Anton Harapi, Lef Nosi."

"I know. But not because of the Jews."

"Go on," said the investigator.

"Well, the question of Jakoel also had to do with local customs. Besides, Fritz von Schwabe was well acquainted with the *Kanun of Lekë Dukagjini*, which we had talked about so often. The Jews of Albania and all the Jews who sought refuge here at that time were considered 'under their hosts' protection', and this principle was inviolable."

Shaqo Mezini leafed through the notes in front him.

The investigators knew everything that had been said at the dinner table that night and asked only one thing. Towards midnight, the dead man, or the supposed Fritz von Schwabe, had said, "You will hear this music differently." What did this phrase mean?

The prisoner furrowed his brow. In fact he did remember this phrase, and even the smile accompanying it, but he had never known what it meant.

"And those private conversations?" said Shaqo Mezini. "You may not believe it but we know about these too." He bent down to the prisoner's right ear to speak softly. "'I'm not Albania, just as you're not Germany, Fritz. We're something else.' Do you remember saying that?"

"Perhaps."

"'We're something else . . . ' A strange claim, isn't it?"

Gurameto hesitated. "I remember some of this but these things, about girls we had known and so forth, weren't important. I remember vaguely . . . But amazingly, this man remembered precisely a dream I had told him long ago. In fact when I was becoming suspicious it was this that persuaded me that the man really was Fritz von Schwabe."

"Go on."

"I had not told this dream to anyone else. In fact it had no particular meaning. It was a kind of nightmare in which I was lying stretched out on the table being operated on by a surgeon who was my own self."

"Aha."

Shaqo Mezini drew close to his ear again. "'When we were students, we said in the tavern . . . but if you are no longer the person you were then.' Do you remember saying those words, doctor?"

The prisoner shook his head.

"What did you say in that tavern?" the investigator went on. "And why should one of you doubt the other?"

Gurameto shook his head again.

"When someone says, 'if you are no longer the person you were then,' I take this as a suspicion that the other person is trying to wriggle out of a duty or agreement."

The prisoner said he couldn't remember. Perhaps they'd been talking about old traditions.

Without hurry or irritation, the investigators put more questions, sometimes mentioning the colonel by name and sometimes calling him "the deceased". What did the deceased say about this, or that? Why did the doctor feel he was on equal terms with the deceased?

The investigators dwelt at great length on this point. "You were a provincial doctor but he was the commander of a tank regiment, and moreover on the victors' side. Where did this sense of equality come from?"

The prisoner shrugged his shoulders.

"I don't know. Memories of student days, perhaps."

"That's not enough," Shaqo Mezini said. "I'll be plain. Who was taking orders from whom?"

"I don't understand."

"We were talking about your courage. Where did it come from?"

The investigation had started to go round in circles.

"This courage to ask for the release of the hostages. Where did you find it?"

"I don't know; perhaps it was because of the dinner."

The prisoner spoke more slowly. "It was due to the reasons you mentioned before, but especially because of the dinner. The invitation seemed the natural thing at the time but later it looked improper."

"What have I done?" he had said on arriving home. His wife and daughter had wondered too. This dinner would require an explanation. Otherwise he would be reviled as a traitor and shot by his own people. The only justification for the dinner would be the release of the hostages.

Now it struck Gurameto as odd that he was no longer being badgered about that great conspiracy, the "Joint". And, more lonely and exhausted than ever, he was overcome by a suspicion. How could they know so much? "How did they find out all this?" he repeated to himself.

Like sheet lightning, pictures flashed through his mind of his wife and daughter, their hair in disarray, raped and tortured amidst cries of "Talk!" "Sprich!" No, it was the cave that caused this fear. These were things that not even his wife and daughter could know. So who did?

Fritz, he thought. Alive, in irons like himself, and under interrogation.

The investigators stared at him as he rejected the idea with a shake of his head.

Then it must be someone else. There could be only one answer. Everybody at the dinner had been under surveillance all the time. They were all suspected by both sides.

With vacant eyes he stared at the investigators as if straining to find out from them, but their own eyes were just as blank.

★

"Bravo! Excellent!"

The delighted investigators were listening to their Russian colleague. Immediately after the session they had gathered in an adjacent cell, which had been turned into an improvised office.

"Ve efferythink know, ha ha ha," laughed the Russian, trying to pronounce the Albanian words. "You were terrific, boys," he went on. "Tell me honestly, did you begin to suspect yourselves that Fritz von Schwabe was alive and in our hands and had told us everything that happened?"

They cheerfully admitted that they had almost been persuaded, even though they knew to the contrary.

"So, let me tell you again, he's dead. Our German colleagues were correct when they told us he died on 11 May in a field hospital in the Ukraine. So, who was 'the deceased'?"

He asked for a coffee with milk before opening the file in front of him with chubby hands. Sipping the coffee, he drew out a sheaf of photographs from the file. "Here is 'the deceased'," he said, pointing to one of them. "Colonel Klaus Hempf, bearer of the Iron Cross. Here he is again, or rather here are the two colonels, the dead one and his ghost, with bandaged heads in a field hospital, in western Ukraine in May 1943. And now here is Klaus Hempf in a place that I think you will recognise."

They gasped. Colonel Klaus Hempf stood smiling in sunglasses, leaning against an armoured vehicle in the city square of Gjirokastër. The statue of Çerçiz Topulli was visible, as was Remzi Kadare's house in the background.

"Incredible," they exclaimed almost in one voice.

"Now, listen carefully," said the Russian.

He briefly recounted the story. The two wounded colonels met by chance in the field hospital in May 1943. Fritz von Schwabe was seriously wounded, a hopeless case, but Klaus Hempf's injuries were less severe. The latter expected to be promoted to general as soon as he was discharged from the hospital and sent to a new front. His colleague was waiting only to die.

It was the sort of deathbed friendship that was common in military hospitals. The officers opened their hearts to each other. The dying man grew nostalgic as his strength ebbed and as he left his last wishes. The colonels shared a common interest in the Balkans. Klaus Hempf was to be transferred there after he left hospital. Fritz von Schwabe had dreamed of such a posting because his bosom friend from university, Gurameto, was there. Both had read the popular novels of Karl May, which extolled the local customs, especially those of the Albanians: hospitality, the word of honour, the *Kanun of Lekë Dukagjini*. Gurameto had often talked about these things.

Clearly Fritz would not be going anywhere and least of all to Albania as he had promised his friend. So he asked his fellow-officer to carry out his dying wish, if destiny led him there: to seek out his friend and bid him farewell. He gave his address: Dr Gurameto, 22 Varosh Street, Gjirokastër.

Klaus promised. It was 11 May 1943. Fritz died, practically in his arms.

Klaus might have forgotten his vow if he had not by chance been in command of the tank regiment entering Albania four months later on 16 September 1943. The name of the city reminded him of his promise. He found the address in his notebook. And so the events as we know them unfolded: his meeting with Dr Gurameto, the sudden whim to present himself as his friend, the invitation and the dinner.

"This sounds like a romantic movie, no?" asked the Russian investigator. "Or a fairy tale. That's what you kept shouting during the interrogation, didn't you? 'What is this fairy tale? What does it mean? Speak!'"

They nodded that this was true.

"But you see, it's no fairy tale. Dr Gurameto is not lying. All this actually happened. This is not speculation or rumour. Our files prove everything."

The Russian investigator now produced from the file some photographs of written pages, extracts from Klaus Hempf's diary. "Does this dinner strike you as mysterious? There is no mystery at all. Here is a record of the conversation, written the next morning with exemplary accuracy."

He also handed over four typed pages.

"You look as if you've seen a ghost. Now take a look at the rubber stamp at the top of each page."

There was the Nazi emblem with the word "Gestapo". Their skin crept more than at the sight of any ghost.

"Didn't it ever occur to you that one of the colonel's aides at the famous dinner would be a Gestapo man? Here are his notes, which we found in the Gestapo archive. You see, we know everything."

The Russian laughed.

"You may ask, so this hero of a colonel was being watched? Of course he was. At that time everybody was suspected of something. You didn't become a suspect; you were one already. But now after the good news here comes the bad. In some cases we don't know everything, and this is one of them."

He sipped the last of his coffee.

"There is one vital element we don't know, and that is why Colonel Klaus Hempf, there on the city square, did not tell Dr Gurameto that he brought a message from his college friend, but said that he himself was Fritz von Schwabe."

For a moment he pinned the two Albanians in his stare.

"Was it a whim? Of course it was. Hempf's personal file describes him as an impulsive, even unreliable character. It's a characteristic of these headstrong, reckless types. But we don't know the real reason behind this caprice. The riddle remains unsolved and this mystery lies behind the dinner. How can we find out this secret?"

He requested a second cup of coffee and continued as the others listened in silence.

"The authors of this conundrum now lie dead and buried."

The Albanian investigators listened in bewilderment.

"They took the truth to their graves," the Russian added. "But before we ask how we can dig up this truth, we must ask ourselves if we need it. Dr Gurameto talked about the German strategy for this country, secret agreements and the like. At the time these things were important but now they are merely the politics of a bygone era. Albania is now a communist country. This story is finished. But let me say again, there is a mystery behind this dinner. From the moment that the German colonel introduces himself as a visitor from the next world, we are in the dark. Now, listen carefully to me."

★

The atmosphere was heavy on that night of 27 February 1953. Shaqo Mezini could not sleep. Lightning was bad for sleep, he had heard. He stood up several times and went to the window, watching the jagged forks above the prison. He had not seen such lightning for a long time. It was called false lightning, he remembered. His thoughts whirred compulsively. What if the wire of the lightning conductor breaks? He imagined the lightning carried into the depths of the prison, down to the Cave of Sanisha, and Gurameto burned to a cinder.

It was almost midnight. He seized his winter coat that lay thrown across the chair, silently descended the stairs and went out into the street.

The staff car of the Interior Ministry was waiting at the end of the alley, with Arian Ciu inside. They muttered a greeting to each other. "What a night!" said his colleague. The car climbed the street with difficulty.

"Dr Gurameto, we have thought a lot about your case."

"What?" said Arian Ciu in a tired voice.

"Nothing. Was I talking to myself?"

"That's what it seemed to me."

Shaqo Mezini had thought about what he would say. "Dr Gurameto, we believe that you have been honest with us in this investigation. You have ideals. We're cut from the same cloth as yourself. We have ideals, but different ones to yours. Fortunately we agree on one thing and that is the importance of the nation. You're convinced that you're helping the nation in what you do. We think the same. Both sides can't be right. It's you or us, Dr Gurameto. Let's find out which it will be.'

The engine noise changed and they noticed they had

entered the castle. The scattered lights barely illuminated the arched vaults. Shaqo Mezini turned over in his mind the same thoughts that had preoccupied him for the last thirty hours.

"We could take the shortest route and convict you on the spot. Collaboration with the occupier. The people are shedding blood on the battlefield against the enemy while you host dinners with music and champagne. That would be sufficient for a bullet in the neck in any country, even France or England.

"We could take it further. Let's go back to the dinner; what was it for? To celebrate treason and toast the German invasion? How shocking. But it could be still worse. Something else might be behind it. Some horror manifesting itself at your dinner. Something that would appal even the Germans. Something monstrous that is bigger than any of us."

Shouts of "Halt!" came from the guards, then the prison's outer gates creaked. A soldier holding an oil lamp lit up the investigators' faces. Then the car proceeded across the deserted courtyard.

"What were we talking about? Your sentence. Hundreds of people heard the music coming from your dinner. The most obvious thing would be to shoot you and intern your wife and daughter. Your story would end on a sandbank by the river. But we have another idea. We have faith in your vein of idealism and we think that you can do something for the nation. The evening before last, you talked to us about the pro-German elite, which included Mehdi Frashëri, Father Anton Harapi, Eqrem Çabej, Lasgush Poradeci, Mustafa Kruja and, if I recollect rightly, Ernest Koliqi. Even though they all made or were about to make the wrong choice, their purpose was, as you said, to serve an ideal. They sacrificed all they had, their reputation, their honour, in a mistaken cause. One sacrificed his Franciscan habit and another his own talent. But they were thinking of the nation. Big Dr Gurameto, that is all we are asking of you. Do what they did."

The car stopped with a jolt.

The inner gates creaked louder than the outer pair. The investigators walked in silence behind the guard, who led them down the long vaulted passage. They found Gurameto huddled on a straw mattress. They helped him to sit up on a chair at the table and brought him coffee with milk.

"Thank you," said the prisoner in German.

It took him some time to collect himself.

It was hard for Shaqo Mezini too. His head felt as heavy as lead. He recited, like a monologue learned by heart, the greater part of what had been running through his mind for the last thirty hours. When he came to the words, "Do what they did", he had a sudden mental block.

The prisoner looked at him helplessly, uncomprehending.

"What the hell," the investigator said to himself, and leafed through the file at random. A short letter in German caught his eye.

"What do you say to this?" he said quietly, handing it to the prisoner.

Gurameto took it from him with a shaking hand.

"This is from my Jewish colleague. This is the second time you've asked me."

"Of course. The letter was intercepted by Soviet intelligence."

Shaqo Mezini read the translated text for the umpteenth time. "My dear colleague, what has happened to you? I have had no news from you since I arrived in Jerusalem. How are you? Have they bothered you because of me? Please write. My heartfelt greetings, Jakoel."

What the hell, Shaqo Mezini thought again. What was the relevance of this letter to what he wanted to say? His memory had never failed him like this before. This bloody doctor had worn him out.

"Do what they did," he said again. This was where he had got stuck. He held his head in the palm of his hand.

"I've got it," he almost exclaimed aloud. His train of thought came back to him. He was talking about the dinner. Of course, that was where it all began. That was the riddle. Nobody could penetrate its innermost depths, its darkest recesses, not all the investigators of the communist camp, not even the Nazis in their day. Not Colonel Klaus Hempf, nor Gurameto himself.

This mystery loomed above everything, and its roots ran deep. Political regimes fell and states were overthrown but the spores of this organism survived. The "Joint" was one of them. The participants themselves did not understand how far it stretched. Murder was only part of its activities. Would Hitler have been a target? His turn might have come. Do something for your country.

All the communist secret services had been on the trail of the "Joint". Stalin was waiting. Did Dr Gurameto understand what this meant? That Stalin himself was waiting . . .

Let Dr Gurameto make this sacrifice for his country.

Sooner or later, the "Joint" would be exposed. Let it be Albania's destiny to do this. Let Albania unmask it and become the golden boy of the bloc, of Stalin himself.

Shaqo Mezini was exhausted. The prisoner's face showed not the slightest comprehension. The investigators tried to calm themselves. In cold, precise terms they told Gurameto what they expected of him. A simple thing, a confession. In other words, a signature, admitting he was a member of the "Joint", as no doubt he was. Just like his old college friend, Fritz von Schwabe and the other colonel, Klaus Hempf. And Little Dr Gurameto, who had already signed.

He had no reason to stare at them like that. He had said it himself during the famous dinner. "I'm not Albania. Just as you're not Germany. We're something else."

"You were members of the 'Joint', Jews, Germans, Albanians, Hungarians. You held your meetings everywhere. The meeting in Albania was just one in a series."

The investigators interrupted one another in their haste.

"You were everywhere. Like the plague."

Everybody knew about the Zionist "Joint" and felt its presence, but it was invisible to the eye. Only Gurameto could see it, only he could fathom the unfathomable. He could explain this dinner and illuminate its dark void. So they could finally get out of this cave. "Talk, you . . . de—"

Whether they pronounced the word "devil" before they saw the shackled man shake his head or just afterwards, they could not tell, neither then nor later. They recollected only a scream of "It's finished!" after which Shaqo Mezini held on to his colleague to keep himself upright.

At three in the morning they gave the order for the prisoner to be put to torture.

★

When dawn broke the torture was still continuing. People came and went through the chambers of the cave like ghosts. The shouts of the torturers were heard, interspersed with Gurameto's groans. "The name of the chief. His nickname. Your cover name. The secret code. Talk!"

The tapping of a cane was heard in the semi-darkness. It must be Blind Vehip who for some reason they had brought there, only to take him away again.

The shouts were gruff, unvarying. "After Stalin, who? Where? You? When? With poison? Radiation? Talk!"

The mournful strains of a gypsy song were heard from somewhere. Shaqo Mezini remembered the day when his fiancée had left him. He had heard a song like this in the distance. He could not remember the words but they more or less went "You said farewell to me/But not to my knife in your heart."

CHAPTER TWELVE

He had the feeling that this was not the first time he had dreamed of Sanisha. She seemed composed and aloof, especially towards himself. Finally she set aside her indifference and, turning her pale face towards him asked, "Is your investigation about me?"

Shaqo Mezini shrugged his shoulders, which seemed to him the best he could do. It was a kind of answer that combined an apology (he was only doing his job) with a feeble protest (an investigation in your cave doesn't necessarily mean it's about you).

She was not at all angry, but not grateful either. In different circumstances this ravished woman might have opened her heart to him. "Officer, if you only knew what they did to me." But she remained cold and distant.

He heard the indistinct buzz of conversation around him. There was a double door through which he could see sparkling chandeliers and people moving to and fro. He heard the name of Stalin, but it seemed to him improper to ask what was happening. Then he understood: Comrade Stalin was hosting a dinner in the Kremlin. Journalists were relaying the news. "Comrade Stalin, on this occasion . . .

All communists should know that the peoples of the world owe a debt . . . "

Sanisha appeared again among the guests. "I don't care," she said to Shaqo Mezini, "but I'm sure my brother won't like it. No brother wants his sister's rape investigated." The investigator shrugged his shoulders again. He wanted to ask if she was invited to Comrade Stalin's dinner. Comrade Stalin, the Father of the Peoples. Then she said, "Perhaps you're no longer frightened of my brother, Ali Pasha Tepelene. In my day, everybody was terrified of him."

It was the sort of dream that you could, with a little effort, snap yourself out of. Shaqo Mezini forced it away but it lingered in his mind. Even after he opened his eyes he could hear the words, "Comrade Stalin, Comrade Stalin, the glorious leader."

He leaped out of bed and ran to the window. Even before flinging the window open, he identified the source of his torment. The voice came from a huge loudspeaker on top of the castle. You did not need to hear the words to know this meant bad news. Loudspeakers did not broadcast anything else. The words came distorted, fragmentary. "At this hour of trial, when Comrade Stalin is suffering . . ."

At least he's not dead, Shaqo Mezini thought.

On the street, as he ran towards the Interior Ministry's branch office, he heard the broadcast distinctly from another direction. It was a bulletin on the patient's condition. "Breathing difficulties . . . intermittent . . ."

He sprinted across the office yard. His colleague Arian Ciu, with a pale, waxen face, was trying to make a phone call. "All the lines are engaged," he said with a guilty look.

Shaqo Mezini, short of breath, did not reply. "Are there any instructions?" he finally gasped.

A short call had come from headquarters in Tirana. "Everybody at their post. This is an order." There was no further explanation.

"At our posts," Shaqo Mezini thought. "Of course."

An inscrutable expression crossed Arian Ciu's face.

"No more?" Shaqo Mezini asked. The lines had been busy for the past hour. "Is the chief in his office?"

"Yes. Our enemies are rejoicing too soon. That was all he said."

"Are you scared?" Shaqo Mezini asked suddenly.

Arian Ciu did not know where to look. "No. What do you mean by that?"

Shaqo Mezini was overcome by a wave of emotion he had never felt before, a barely resistible urge to lay his head on the chest of his office colleague, and say, "Hold on to me, brother. We're both lost."

The door opened noisily. The chief of investigations entered, stared at them as if surprised to find them there, and just as noisily departed again.

They stood in silence and looked towards the window. It gradually dawned on them that they were both looking in the direction of the military airport. How incredible to think back to the time when the investigators from Berlin and Moscow had landed there.

At midday the station chief held a short meeting in his office. The latest bulletin reported no change in Stalin's condition. The orders from headquarters remained the same: everybody at their posts. The radio was broadcasting classical music and two of the typists were in tears.

At four in the afternoon Shaqo Mezini jumped to his feet. His face glowered. "Get up," he said to his colleague. "Let's go."

"Where?"

"You know where."

Without a word to anybody and with unsteady steps they set off for the prison. Sometimes the noise of their footsteps seemed too much to bear and the cobbles cracked explosively under their boots, and sometimes the sound was muffled, as if they were walking on clouds.

In the Cave of Sanisha they found Gurameto stretched out as usual on his straw mattress. He did not move when they entered or even when they called his name. The marks of torture were clearly visible on his cheeks.

"So you're pleased at this, are you?" said Shaqo Mezini. "You heard Stalin is ill and you're pleased at this, scum."

He was still short of breath from the hurried ascent and he could barely utter the words.

"He can hardly breathe, and this makes you happy, doesn't it?"

A faint gleam in Gurameto's eyes suggested to the investigator that medical curiosity was one of the few instincts that the doctor retained. The investigator tried to conceal his own shortness of breath but this made it worse. The imprisoned doctor had probably taken what he said about breathing to refer to himself, not Stalin.

"Stalin can hardly breathe, do you hear me?" he shouted. "He's dying and you're glad, is that right?"

The prisoner did not reply.

The investigator's eyes wandered to the corner where the old instruments of torture glinted dully. He remembered a few years ago a British collector, who was fond of Albania, wanting to buy them for pounds sterling.

Arian Ciu was looking at them too. "For what other occasion were these tools intended," Mezini thought.

But he surprised himself by saying something else. "Gurameto, you're a doctor. You can't be pleased when someone is barely breathing, can you?" He brought his face close to the prisoner and continued in a whisper. "You would like to cure him, wouldn't you? Speak!"

He thought he saw the man nod, but he could not be sure.

"Dr Gurameto," he said gently. "You have it in your power to cure Stalin."

He drew close to the man's head again and murmured into his right ear. A word from him, or rather, his signature at the end of the record of interrogation would perform the miracle. It was said that it was worry over the failure to expose the Jewish plot that had laid Stalin low. So, the news that the plot had been exposed would surely restore him to life. "Save Stalin, doctor," Shaqo Mezini gasped.

The other investigator watched dumbfounded.

Shaqo Mezini was close to collapse. Like his voice, his knees were giving way. His ribs were melting like candle wax and could no longer contain his heart. He felt an overpowering desire to hold the prisoner in his arms, to weep with him.

Did he fall to his knees now, or had it been some time ago? With a trembling, beseeching hand, he held out the document. "Bring him back to life," he said tenderly. "Stalin's resurrection is more important than Christ's. Raise Stalin from the grave!"

This final plea exhausted him completely.

Both men watched the prisoner, making no movement.

This time Shaqo Mezini thought he saw Gurameto shake his head. "No!" the investigator screamed to himself, holding his hands to his eyes, as if blinded.

The next day in the office the hours crept wearily past. First one man and then the other looked into the distance towards the small military airport. They knew they were waiting in vain but their heads automatically made the same movement.

During the afternoon the phone calls petered out. Not just the office but the whole country seemed stricken. Arian Ciu stepped out occasionally to the next-door offices in search of news but each time came back without a word. The order was still the same: everybody at their posts. It became a catchphrase.

After his tiring night, Shaqo Mezini could not keep his mind focused. The desolate appearance of the airport depressed him more than anything else and reminded him of another dream, about how he might become one of the "high-flyers". He had been struck when he saw the German investigator descending the aircraft steps in his casually unzipped leather jacket, his scarf blowing in the wind. He would have liked to look like this, the socialist camp's famous investigator landing at airports in Budapest, Moscow and Sofia, in pursuit of the common enemy. He remembered the familiar exhilaration of times like this, which he associated in his mind with a particular song.

We are sons of Stalin
Prepared to do and die
Until the hammer and sickle
O'er every land does fly.

Now this dream, like the Great Man's breathing, was ebbing. It was like that afternoon long ago when he had come home after a tedious meeting and his mother, with a bewildered expression, had handed him a letter left by his fiancée. "Don't try to understand why. There's no going back."

And so it turned out. She never came back and he never found out the reason why. Sometimes he suspected himself of avoiding the truth. At home, whenever his fiancée was mentioned, he saw an unspoken question in his mother's eyes. How can this son of mine, who uncovers everyone's secrets, fail to understand his own mistake?

After the arrest of the two Gurametos, when their entire list of patients was screened, Shaqo Mezini was horrified to see not only his mother's name but his fiancée's. Numb with shock, he carefully checked the dates. Her appointment was three months after their engagement and five weeks after they had first slept together. Obsessively, he asked himself the reason for this visit and why she had kept it secret from him.

During the first investigation of Big Dr Gurameto, his eyes drifted involuntarily to the doctor's right hand, the one that performed gynaecological examinations.

He pictured that silent afternoon when she had left the house with bowed head to go to the hospital, who could tell why.

He would have given anything to know the truth.

A week later he happened to find himself alone with the prisoner, against all regulations. He had never broken a rule before, but his conscience was easy. This infraction did no harm to the State.

He spoke quietly to the prisoner, as if at a routine interrogation of an ordinary suspect. He mentioned his fiancée's name and added that she was a young woman of twenty-four. According to the hospital register she had attended her appointment at four thirty on the afternoon of 17 February 1951.

The prisoner had furrowed his brow and said that he couldn't remember her.

She was an ordinary-looking woman of medium build. The doctor shook his head again.

"Try to remember, doctor," said Shaqo Mezini, noticing with alarm his own altered voice. The anxiety of those unforgotten weeks flooded over him again. "Doctor, please," he entreated in a muffled voice. "Tell me out of human kindness . . . she was my fiancée."

The prisoner made no sign.

"You don't remember? Of course you don't. She wouldn't strike you in any way. She was an ordinary woman. She was no great beauty."

Shaqo Mezini sat down and his voice became colder and more threatening. "Why did she come to you? Why shouldn't I know the reason? Did she complain about me? Speak!"

The prisoner still sat speechless.

"At least tell me what was wrong with her. Just listen to me. What was the problem?"

"I can't remember."

"Really?"

"Even if she did come to me, I wouldn't tell you. It's a matter of confidentiality."

"Monster," Shaqo Mezini said to himself. "Heartless monster. Hun."

At all the later sessions he tried to avert his eyes from the prisoner's right hand.

On 3 March before dawn he had given the order for the prisoner to be put to torture. He had gone to the chief operative named Tule Balloma. "Listen, there's something on my mind. Those two fingers, the index finger and the next one, what do you call it. Give them a good twist."

The operative looked at him strangely. "There are other parts that hurt more, boss."

"I know, I know," he had replied. "But it's those I want. Crush them good and proper."

"Don't worry, boss. You'll see."

He was curious to see the result, although it would be small consolation.

For two years he had brooded on his fiancée's desertion. He never imagined that just at the time when the scar was healing, the investigation of the doctors would lay bare this wound again. When they had assigned him to this case its global dimensions had staggered him. Simultaneously there came a pang: it was too late. If this had come earlier perhaps his fiancée would not have left him. The file contained something for which he had subconsciously yearned, the promise of celebrity.

The Dzerzhinsky Academy, which of all institutions should have cultivated an indifference to fame and the charms of women, surreptitiously offered these inducements. Forbidden lust haunted the cadets' nightly dreams. Their officers, who knew every secret, could not fail to understand this, but astonishingly, instead of discouraging these desires, they openly hinted that they could hold the entire world in their hands if they knew how to reach out for it. The sons of Stalin would drown the world in blood. The world with its temples, cathedrals, its men and glamorous women, would kneel before them.

His fiancée had proved resistant to this fantasy. At the first supper at her home, supposedly by accident, he had let her see his pistol as he took off his jacket, but to no effect. She had shown no curiosity but only an obvious disdain for firearms.

His eventual fame would no doubt change this and he would become attractive to women, like the commissars with their leather jackets and scars on their foreheads. Or the surgeons who knew how to handle them. If only he too could be somebody. The young Ali Pasha Tepelene supposedly said that if he had been vezir, he would not have allowed the men of Kardhiq to ravish his sister, and from that day his sole ambition had been to become vezir, to take his revenge.

Shaqo Mezini seemed about to become a star at the precise moment in his life when it was of no use to him. He had known this instinctively as soon as he heard the radio broadcasts about the plot, when the newspapers with their banner headlines arrived, and later, as he watched the German investigator striding across the windswept tarmac to the airport building. Later, fame seemed to draw a little closer every day and came almost within his grasp, as it had on those heady evenings at the Dzerzhinsky Academy. Dozens of his student friends from Berlin to Ulan Bator were no doubt at the same time investigating the same repellent case. But destiny shone more brightly on him than on anyone else. His dream of becoming the most famous investigator of the socialist camp was about to become a reality: Shaqo Mezini, the thirty-year-old Albanian sleuth. There would be interviews, meetings with young pioneers and congress delegations. "Comrade Stalin, this is Shaqo Mezini, who exposed the famous 'Joint'." Then Stalin would invite him to supper and perhaps even talk to him tête-à-tête.

His intoxicated imagination stopped short before this climax. He was content to leave the details vague. At times, the scene of another supper threatened to superimpose itself, Christ's perhaps. He knew about this from the Bible, which he had read and even underlined in red pencil while investigating Father Foti, the priest of Varosh. But more than anything else he remembered Gurameto's dinner, which had started it all. He saw himself present sometimes as the man who was to arrest the mysterious guest and sometimes as this very guest himself, the all-powerful visitant from the grave.

Don't give up, he thought. There is still hope.

It was 4 March and Stalin was still alive. Towards dawn they tortured Gurameto again. The operatives were sure he would sign.

The day was overcast with frozen clouds shot through with a deceptive light. The radio carried classical music interspersed with listeners' letters and statements from meetings of workers and soldiers. Wishes for a speedy recovery, threats to our enemies.

The verses published in the press all mentioned Stalin's laboured breathing. Everybody thought he was at his last gasp.

Gurameto's torture continued till dawn. The investigators no longer waited for anybody's instructions. Late in the afternoon they searched his house again and seized his gramophone and records. Among them they found Schubert's "Death and the Maiden", mentioned in the statements. They played it while the torture continued.

For the prophecy to be fulfilled, the dead colonel's words had to come true. "'You'll hear this music differently.' Do you remember him saying that?"

Shaqo Mezini rambled as if in a fever. Arian Ciu listened to him impassively, alarmed by his colleague's recourse to the Bible.

After two hours they both went to the hospital to fetch the surgical instruments that Gurameto had brought from Germany, each one with the initial "G" engraved on it. Arian Ciu did not need his colleague to explain that they would torture Gurameto with his own tools, to fulfil the other prophecy, seen in his dream, that he would be operated on with his own scalpels.

CHAPTER THIRTEEN

The news of Stalin's death was broadcast shortly before noon. Shaqo Mezini was lying half-dressed on his bed after a strenuous night in the Cave of Sanisha when he felt his mother's hand touch his shoulder. "Shaqo, Shaqo," she said in a low voice. "Get up! He's dead."

He leaped to his feet, seized first his revolver from the bedhead and then his overcoat, bounded down the stairs in twos and threes and ran out into the street.

"Louder!" he thought, without knowing whom he might be addressing. His feet carried him instinctively to the office of the Interior Ministry. His mind was vacant. Then he realised that he had been talking to the loudspeaker. It was not blaring as loud as it should, nor did the mountains of Lunxhëria look sufficiently sombre. "Bad news for me," he thought.

At the office his heartbeat steadied. All his comrades were there. With bloodshot eyes and without a word, they embraced each other as they arrived, as if at a funeral. He wrapped his arms round Arian Ciu's neck and could not suppress a sob.

A hundred yards away the same was happening at the Party Committee. Decorated war veterans, angrily red-eyed, stood in groups in front of the door. Couriers entered the building, only to emerge with even grimmer expressions than before.

At one o'clock a collective wail from the children went up from the yard of the primary school. Many people could stand it no longer and fled, shutting themselves up in their homes. Others who had taken to their beds during Stalin's long illness struggled to rise from them.

That afternoon people gathered in public halls and courtyards to listen together to the radio broadcast of the rally of mourning from the capital. The announcer's trembling voice described the scene in Skanderbeg Square in Tirana, where the nation's leaders knelt in front of the dead man's statue. In a halting voice the Leader swore eternal loyalty on behalf of all Albanian communists.

Some people fainted and were carried to the hospital. By the post office, Remzi Kadare, roaring drunk, pointed a finger at the emergency entrance. Amid his sobs of despair, he was telling a story that his listeners took to be about the big event of the day, but was in fact his recollection of the fatal poker game when he had lost his house.

On other streets could be heard the shouts of unfortunate people as they were dragged by the hair to the Interior Ministry, accused of having laughed at the memorial rally instead of crying, although they swore blind they hadn't been laughing at all but were as broken-hearted as everybody else. But for some reason their weeping had turned into a snigger. They were beaten all the harder.

After the rally Shaqo Mezini told his colleague that his legs would not carry him any longer and he was leaving. They could call for him if necessary.

At home he collapsed into a leaden sleep. When he woke up it was dark. He had a momentary sensation of being suspended in a void, above a kind of abyss of grief and fear. Stalin was gone. He no longer had . . . What else could he have? Speak!

He shook his head, assailed by a cruel and unexpected recollection of the white stomach of his fiancée and the dark regions beneath her garters. He felt a pang at having had so little chance to savour them.

The pain ripped through his chest and the scream he suppressed was more violent than the one that came from his throat. His idol Stalin was no longer in this world; worse, his enemy Gurameto still was.

What could be more unjust? Shaqo Mezini shuddered with a strange fear at the prospect of being left alone in this world of sorrows with this monster Gurameto. It was unthinkable. He imagined the doctor's cynical smile. "He's gone, your little father's gone, he's left you all." And his flesh crept again.

No, he thought. Never.

With uncertain steps he left the house. The streets were deserted. A street lamp flickered but refused to die. The Interior Ministry building was in semi-darkness. The guard on night duty looked at him in pity. In the office he found a note from Arian Ciu, "I'm at home. Call me if anything happens."

A short time later the two men's boots were heard, scraping against the cobbles on the street up to the castle. Neither of them spoke; it appeared that first one man and then the other were sleepwalking. They climbed for a long time, as if through clouds. Shaqo Mezini thought he saw the other man's boots strike sparks, like the hooves of a horse he had once seen in childhood struggling to climb the cobbled street.

The iron gates to the Cave of Sanisha creaked dolefully. Gurameto was lying just as they had left him, stretched out on the straw.

Shaqo Mezini touched his knees with the toecap of his boot. "Wake up, Stalin's dead!" The prisoner's expression did not change under the pale light of the torch. The black patches and smears of dried blood gave his face the appearance of a crudely painted mask.

"This makes you laugh, eh?"

The mask did not change. Its expression could mean anything: laughter, grief, entreaty, anger, menace. ("When he heard the news of Stalin's death, he laughed. Before my very eyes. I lost it. I couldn't control myself.")

The investigator's eyes wandered from his face to his bandaged hand. ("No, I was not trying to destroy evidence. I didn't know his fingers had been cut off.")

Silently he motioned to Arian Ciu and the two started to drag the prisoner by the feet.

The empty handcuff on the prisoner's right hand clanged as it hit the floor.

"Where's the other one?" Shaqo Mezini asked.

"Who?"

"The other one, I said. The little doctor."

"There's no other doctor."

Shaqo Mezini stopped in his tracks. His expression had never looked so menacing.

"I mean . . . they've been separated for several days, you know."

Their voices echoed indistinctly in the long vaulted

passage. Where? How? Perhaps he was in the next chamber.

The superintendent of the cave joined them.

"He's been in that room for a while. The young trainees beat him. You know better than I do . . . The first-year intake."

In each chamber their voices sounded different.

"Maybe he was shot by mistake," the superintendent continued. "There's been a lot of confusion in the last few days, believe me."

Some of the chambers were pitch dark. In one, two points of light danced like cat's eyes.

"What are those sparks?" asked the investigators.

"It's Blind Vehip," the superintendent replied guiltily. "The lads were making fun of him. They stuck phosphorescent stones in his eye sockets."

"How do they find time for things like that?"

"One of the cave guards was telling me about it. I think they just found this guy," Arian Ciu said.

"He's a goner," the superintendent said, throwing the beam of his torch onto Blind Vehip's face.

"It doesn't look like him," Shaqo Mezini said. "Never mind. Big deal: Put him in that other handcuff."

"That needs a signature here," the superintendent said in a voice of entreaty, stretching out a piece of paper.

Shaqo Mezini did not reply. His hands were still occupied.

When he felt the other man tied to his wrist, Dr Gurameto gave the first signs of life. He was trying to say something.

"Don't get me into trouble, boss," said the superintendent.

The investigator looked at him with contempt. "Stalin's dead! Don't you understand that? It's chaos everywhere."

"I know," the superintendent replied in a sheepish voice. "But what's a poor man like me to do? Rules are rules."

They were close to the entrance to the cave, and felt the cold night air.

"Here," the superintendent said, pointing to a place on the sheet of paper. "'Reason for prisoner's removal: visit to crime scene'."

Much later Big Dr Gurameto's final hours were reconstructed with considerable accuracy from the record of the autopsy, the two judicial files and the testimonies of Arian Ciu, the superintendent of the Cave of Sanisha and the driver. The statements of Shaqo Mezini and Blind Vehip were not taken into account because of the confused mental state of both men.

All the facts agreed that towards dawn on 6 March 1953, more precisely at three forty in the morning, the prison car left the yard with five people inside: the two investigators, the driver and the two prisoners. It passed through the yard and the main gate of the castle and took the road leading out of the city.

For a long time there was silence in the car and the prisoners gave no sign of life. Then the cold night air revived Big Dr Gurameto and he tried to say something. Because of his lack of teeth his words were indistinct, so nobody paid him any attention. The other prisoner made no sound.

On the highway, when the car passed the cemetery of Vasiliko, Dr Gurameto came to life again. He tried to ask for something, more insistently than before, pointing with his free hand to the cemetery wall. But still nobody listened to him. A few hundred yards further on, he gestured again. After that, nothing worth noting happened until they reached the sandbank by the river.

The experts went back countless times to the short period when the car sped along this stretch of road but could shed no light on this most mysterious moment of all when Gurameto was trying to attract attention. All the witnesses reported him making incoherent noises but none of them could offer any explanation.

Of Gurameto's three attempts to speak, the experts were able to interpret only the first. Probably the first thing that Big Dr Gurameto understood when he came round was that the person handcuffed to him was not his colleague. Evidently he was trying to say so. "This isn't the other doctor." Or, "This man is dead."

No explanation could be found for his other two efforts to communicate, when he had been even more insistent and almost violent, waving his arm in the direction of the cemetery. The answer to the mystery seemed to lie in this gesture.

The statements described convincingly and consistently his final moments after the car reached the river at the place known as the Brigand's Ford. The investigators had pulled the prisoners out of the car while the driver dug a hole in the sand. They carried both prisoners to the edge of the hole and, although they suspected that one of them had been dead for some time, shot both several times with their revolvers.

★

The trial of the two investigators was held towards the end of spring. Shaqo Mezini was sentenced to three and a half months' imprisonment and Arian Ciu to two and a half, both for "misuse of office". The mitigating circumstances of the shock of Stalin's death and especially their victims' cynical response to this dreadful news were decisive in reducing their sentences. Shaqo Mezini, because of his psychological imbalance, completed his sentence in the psychiatric hospital at Vlora, while Arian Ciu served his in the city prison, not far from the Cave of Sanisha.

Both were later reinstated at the Interior Ministry, but only to work in the uniform section of the Procurement Department rather than the Office of Investigations.

The graves were exhumed forty years later in September 1993, shortly after the fall of communism.

Relatives of the deceased found the bodies handcuffed, just as they had been buried. It was discovered first of all that one of the shackled men was not Little Dr Gurameto but someone else who was never identified. Little Dr Gurameto's body was never found, despite his family's persistent efforts. Indeed, the little doctor had left such few and slight traces behind him that some people began to doubt he had ever existed. Further research did not lay these suspicions to rest and indeed only strengthened them. There was no mention of Little Dr Gurameto in the investigation record or the witness statements. Plenty of people believed, even if they did not say so publicly, that Little Dr Gurameto had been merely an exteriorisation or projection of Big Dr Gurameto's unconscious, a projection which the people around him for some inexplicable reason had accepted.

Dr Gurameto's file was opened again fifteen years later in the spring of 2007, when the European Union asked Albania, like all the other countries of the former Eastern Bloc, to punish the crimes of communism.

This time, European as well as Albanian experts examined the case for weeks. Rarely had they been given the chance to get their teeth into such an investigation, which involved the secret services of several countries with entirely different regimes and histories: the royal and later the communist Albanian secret service, the German Gestapo and Stasi and the Soviet and indirectly the Israeli secret services. Moreover, besides such curiosities as the rhymes of Blind Vehip and the confessions of women, who, terrified by the summons to the Investigator's Office, had revealed secrets that they had sworn to take to their graves, the file also included the statements of the surgeon's daughter and his wife. The latter had testified to things that only she could know, such as the doctor's nightmares, and legends such as that of the dead house guest, which his grandmother, as he himself had recalled, had used to lull him to sleep. Among the doctor's several expressions of remorse for things he shouldn't have done, the most important was his sigh, "Ah, that dinner ... " which occasionally escaped him quite unexpectedly.

Even so, the more complicated the file on Dr Gurameto grew, the more lucid it became. With the exception of a brief moment that remained shrouded in mystery, the logic and continuity of the whole were incontestable. This fragment of time was an inconsiderable episode in his life, taking no more than five or six minutes, but it was of such intense opacity that it could have lasted for years.

It concerned the dawn of 6 March 1953, or more precisely the short period when the investigators' car was following the potholed highway alongside the cemetery's perimeter wall. The records showed that only the first of Dr Gurameto's three attempts to speak had been entirely explained. The two others, which were the most frightening, had remained obscure.

What had the prisoner been trying to say? What profound distress suddenly gave him the superhuman strength almost to break out of his handcuffs?

Leafing through the file's innumerable pages, the investigators sometimes thought that they espied a ray of light. This happened especially when they were tired. But any effort of concentration would cause this faint gleam to retreat back into the darkness from which it had emerged, as if it feared exposure.

In time they grasped that this explanation that was on the brink of becoming apparent was less a supernatural sign than something else that had no place in an investigative file. Any investigation would reject it like foreign tissue, not for any esoteric reason but simply because neither investigative skills nor language itself had yet created the terms for explanations of this kind.

There was no evidence anywhere to show what really occurred at the most ineffable moment of Big Dr Gurameto's life at the dawn of that March day.

Here is what happened.

6 March 1953. Towards dawn. The car leaves the prison yard heading out of the city. The prisoners are silent, perhaps even unconscious. The fresh air revives one of them, Big Gurameto. After his first mumbled attempts to protest that he is tied to a stranger, he probably loses consciousness again. He wakes up later on the highway as the car passes the cemetery wall. In the faint reddish light of dawn he recognises the famous Vasiliko graveyard. He has been there dozens of times for the burials of patients who died under his hands on the operating table, or later. But he has another reason to remember this cemetery. When his grandmother, to soothe him to sleep, had told him the tale of the dead man wrongly invited to dinner, he, like many small boys, had pictured himself in the role of the son, whose father, as the legend relates, gave him an invitation to deliver to the first chance passer-by.

The Vasiliko cemetery was the only graveyard he knew, so he had imagined himself running past it, like in the legend. He is scared, his heart shakes, and instead of continuing along the road until he meets a passer-by, he reaches his hand through the cemetery railings to throw the invitation inside. As he flees he turns his head and sees the invitation where it has fallen, lying white on top of a grave.

Now, forty years later, when the prison car passes this cemetery, this vision returns. It seems to him that the invitation, thrown away long ago, is the cause of everything. It is still lying there. He feels an insane desire to turn back and pick up the invitation from the grave where it has fallen, to turn time back and retract the hand of fate, before the dead man can receive the message.

In his distressed state he believes he can do this and so

he gasps, his mouth foams with exertion, and with his free hand he points to the iron railing behind which the white invitation card still rests. But nobody listens to him.

A second vision comes to him a short time later. Now he is no longer six years old, running with an invitation in his hand, but another Gurameto, grown-up, indeed dead, who has rotted in the grave for many years, as he saw himself in a nightmare. The marble grave with the headstone on which his name is carved looms above him, and around the cemetery are the iron railings.

Through these railings a woman's dainty hand with long fingers and a ring with a sad association lets fall an invitation. It flutters forlornly before coming to rest on his grave.

The dead man, that is, Gurameto himself, bewildered after so many silent years, feels compelled to obey the order and rise up to go where he has been invited to dinner. To what dinner? He cannot tell. To the house of that woman whom he recognises and yet does not, or to 22 Varosh Street? To his own dinner, perhaps, the one that caused him so much trouble long ago?

That is the order, but he does not want to obey it. More foam gathers at the corners of his mouth. He screams and strains to break his shackles, until the terrified investigators draw their revolvers. But he will not calm down. Still he struggles to turn back to that grave, to remove that invitation at last and change destiny. But it is impossible.

Mali i Robit (Durrës); Lugano; Paris
Summer–winter, 2007–2008